Just a little some!
~ Sus ♡

THE
MAGNIFICENCE
OF
EDWARD

SUSHEELA KUNDARGI

ISBN: 978-1-6781-0447-4

The Magnificence of Edward is a fictional tale about a tall, timid young man whose life is pleasantly predictable until he unintentionally steps out of his comfort zone and changes his fate by making one seemingly small yet very out-of-character decision. What Edward would easily classify as the worst event of his life thus far transforms into something magical and serendipitous that would never have happened had he stuck to the status quo.

Susheela Kundargi
Vancouver, BC, Canada 2022
First Edition
http://themagnificenceofedward.com

DEDICATION

I dedicate this book firstly to my Children:
Damien Caley, Line, & Rhiannon;
You're three of the sweetest,
Most gentle humans I know;
Secondly, to my clients, past, present, and future:
the answer is in this silly little book;
and lastly, to my friends who encouraged
(read, proofed, and critiqued)
this folly:
Joanne, Monalisa, & Katie.

Choose Happiness.

Create Magic.

Love.

ABOUT THE AUTHOR

Originally from Montreal, QC, Canada, Susheela Kundargi is a multi-disciplined entrepreneur who currently oversees the structure and process of authors' projects that benefit from her background as a ghostwriter and creative consultant.

She has worked extensively as a content creator, curriculum developer, alternative therapist, college instructor, artist and designer, primarily in technology, agriculture, sustainability, film/tv, music, fashion & interior design, and psychology/self-help sectors for over 25 years.

Susheela has ghostwritten, designed, authored, and co-authored books and screenplays and is still actively involved in mentoring and content development.

Living on the unceded territory of the Coast Salish peoples, Tsartlip, Sḵwx̱wú7mesh (Squamish), Selilwitulh (Tsleil-Waututh) and xʷməθkʷəy̓əm (Musqueam) Nations, (British Columbia, Canada) she is an activist for organic farming, food security, indigenous issues, & green initiatives.

Innovation, efficiency, natural living, humour, and compassion are tenets by which she lives.

TABLE OF CONTENTS

CHAPTER ONE

A cluster of spindly toes, poorly coated with black polish, poked up from the dismal bathwater of the pink tub. Grey, desolate bubbles, with a negligible amount of scum, floated on the water's surface. It's not easy for a person of considerable stature to fit in a basin this size. Although the tiles were past their prime, there was a regal, retro elegance to them, if only they were scoured periodically.

Inadequate lighting, a little black mould, a loosely attached soap dish, being privy to the intimate bathroom conversations of the couple who live next-door— this is what $2000 got you nowadays.

Edward adjusted himself in the tub to warm up his chest and shoulders, submerging them in the murky water, which in turn pushed his scrawny knees up like two barren icebergs. His eyeliner and mascara were running down his face, which did little to hide the swollen black eye that was coming into its full splendour. He ran a scraped and recently coagulated bloody hand through his thin spiky hair with wretched vanity while his other hand dangled over the edge, clinging to a mickey of bourbon. It would have been a larger bottle, and he couldn't remember if he had ever tasted bourbon before, but it was all he could afford with what he had left in his pocket that night.

Sparky was pleading with symphonic meows outside the bathroom door. The inch gap at the bottom seemed to amplify more than muffle the broadcast. Edward stared in disdain and intrigue at Sparky's nose visible under the door and the occasional cat arm that would swing through. Sparky stood up, and with one strong push and melodic feline grunt, he forced the door open, pranced in accompanied by a gust of cold air, then perched himself majestically atop of the toilet seat, staring insistently into Edward's eyes.

"What?" Edward asked Sparky in a semi-drunken, defensive way, knowing full well he was being judged by his four-legged ego-driven companion. Sparky just maintained his gaze, but Edward began to shiver. He propped himself up enough to place the bottle on the floor beside him, resigning himself to the fact that his languishing was at an end.

Edward unsteadily rose, reached for his less than clean towel, and proclaimed to Sparky with a sigh and slurred speech, "In hindsight, Sparky old boy, *Goth-Jesus* was not my best costume to date." Sparky said nothing. Edward haphazardly wrapped the towel around himself and closed the door to keep the heat in. The light flickered. "In *fact*," he continued swaying, "or... however... it was the *best* costume for getting the shit kicked out of me". Sparky jumped down from the toilet and begged to be let out, as if utterly ashamed of his master. Edward opened and closed the door with just enough time for Sparky to squeeze his ample orange posterior through it.

"Blessed are the meek, Sparky. And the poor. But they never said anything about the satirical." Edward pressed his forehead to the bathroom door pitifully when he realized his bruises and cuts felt worse than before.

Without moving, Edward's gaze focused on his feet. As he stared down at his toes, he realized that he didn't own any nail polish remover. As chagrined as he was already, the thought of what the medical staff would think of him should he have to present himself at the doctor's office was now overtaking him.

"It'll be fine," Edward reassured himself. "It was Hallowe'en. It's not *that* unusual." Still, despite what he was telling himself, he was fixated on removing the polish as soon as humanly possible.

He remembered that there was a drugstore about eight blocks away that was open all night. He quickly proceeded to drop the towel on the floor and run to his room to minimize the draught against his luminescent, vulnerable body.

Although generally not the neatest of housekeepers, he was more careless than usual, rummaging through his underwear drawer, speedily pulling up the warmest pair of briefs he could find. He topped it all off with an arbitrary sweatshirt and a fresh pair of jeans from a laundry basket at the foot of his bed. Edward could feel the alcohol buzz wearing off as he struggled with his mismatched socks. As he was standing up, eager to get out and back home, he caught a glimpse of himself in the mirror. Sparky sat on the dresser, patiently observing and most certainly judging.

"Jesus!" Edward gasped, "I look like shit." Sparky meowed in agreement. For a moment, Edward contemplated not going back out. He stood frozen in hesitation for a solid three seconds as every eventuality remarkably ran through his mind, only to leave him satisfied with going once again.

Outside, it had become so cold that Edward could now see his breath. He felt the chilly air was surprisingly welcome on his painfully bruised face, and he hoped that it would reduce the swelling by the time he reached the store. The streets were sparsely populated, and Edward was pleased that he wouldn't have to be seen by anyone. In fact, it looked like the few people he was encountering were equally disinterested in him and were all rushing to get out of the cold.

Edward's confidence was resuming while he shuffled quickly with his hands in his pockets, and he could see the excessively bright drugstore lights ahead. Mild optimism returned, and he hardly felt abnormal in any way. Edward checked both ways before crossing the virtually empty street and skipped onto the sidewalk at the drugstore. The cars parked along the way were there for the night with the windows already frosted. He could see only a few people inside and gallantly trotted in, forgetting for the moment how unsightly his face was.

Rushing past each aisle, mumbling as he read the overhead signage aloud, jumped from one aisle to the next, "No, that's not it, that's not it, feminine hygiene and –" without forewarning, a mousy young woman in a lab coat was standing there facing him. In her own vacant way, she looked startled. Edward's eyes darted to her bright blue name tag, "Hilda." He stared back at her pallid, expressionless face; she stared back at him like an obscure and exotic bird.

"Uhh… I'm looking for," he started but was abruptly interrupted by the deep deadpan voice of Hilda, "First Aid, aisle 7". She never blinked, but Edward was warmly reminded of his disfigurement. Warm being the initial sensation which escalated quickly to burning— partially due to the cold wearing off and expedited by embarrassment. "uh— oh no, no, I am looking for uh… you know, the stuff that takes off, um…" Hilda stared patiently unamused. Edward continued, "The stuff to remove nail polish, from— nail polish remover." Unintentionally, he ended the sentence to sound like a question.

Hilda finally squeezed out one solid and firm blink, "*Acetone,*" she emphasized, "is in the nail polish section, beside the makeup towards the front." She steadily walked past Edward to complete whatever she had set out to do before their awkward encounter. "Acetone! Right!" Edward whispered excitedly, then ran over to the correct section.

There was a staggering number of options in this product category, distressing Edward further. All he wanted was a simple solution. He squatted down to read the various labels of acetone on the bottom shelf.

"Fake or real?" boomed a deep, gravelly voice beside him, almost making Edward topple backward. As Edward recovered his throbbing heart from the dusty floor, he looked up at the man standing beside him. "Pardon me?" Edward asked as he sprung to his feet in one swift motion. The rotund, burly, bearded man in his late 50s elaborated slowly for Edward's benefit, "Fake nails or real nails?"

Baffled, Edward replied to the absurdity of the question, "Real nails," again sounding proudly uncertain.

The man continued, commiserating, "My wife sends me here to get all *sorts* of things. The thing is, if she's got fake nails and you get the regular stuff, it *destroys* them. But if you get the stuff for fake nails, an' she's got real nails, it does fuck all. Personally, I use it to erase permanent marker from plastic and metal."

Edward, mouth gaping, now completely taken aback, with more information than he ever thought he would need to know about nail polish remover, felt appreciatively relieved, if not comforted by this grizzly yet knowledgeable fellow.

With a few quick grunts, the man bent down, snatched up the no-name brand acetone and presented it to Edward. "This'll do ya." Edward promptly took the bottle, desperate to get home, "Thanks, man," and proceeded to the check-out.

Only one cashier was open, and Edward ran up behind a teenager with a foot-high, spiky, red mohawk who was buying a 6-pack of caffeinated drinks and paying in coins. He momentarily lost track of his counting and looked back at Edward apologetically. Normally, Edward would keep his opinions to himself, but for whatever reason, he said, "Those aren't good for you, you know?" without missing a beat, the boy agreed, "yeah, I know, I have an essay to do" and shrugged it off. The male cashier, who looked like he could be Hilda's brother, stared irritatingly at Edward.

Once the boy had counted out every bit of change, the teller let out a big sigh without looking up, "Bag?" Anticipating the answer to be 'no,' he scooped all the coins into his hand and then methodically dropped them into their allotted compartments in the till.

"Next!" he shouted as he slammed the drawer shut. By now, an elderly lady about 4'11" was standing behind Edward. He placed the nail polish remover on the counter. "a dollar ninety-seven," announced the cashier, unaffected in any way by the purchase. Edward handed him eight quarters, which was everything he had taken from his clean jacket.

Content, Edward headed home, carrying his acetone. His steps had a light-hearted nonchalance about them. He entered the lobby of his apartment building only to encounter the young woman from 3a. He didn't recognize her at first due to her vixenesque Hallowe'en costume. He stood next to her at the elevator doors and pressed the button even though it was already lit.

She turned to him and started, "Oh my god! What happened to you?" she sounded genuinely concerned despite being someone who he previously determined was clearly out of his league, ran in different circles, and that sort of thing. The elevator doors opened, and Edward being the gentleman he was, motioned to Elisa to enter before him. "Ah, it's nothing, really," he brushed it off because he was still far too humiliated to recount the tale as he pressed the 3 and 4 on the panel. However, she persisted, "But it looks awful! Oh my god! What happened?"

As the elevator was just passing the second floor, Edward conceded, "I'll tell you about it some other time." Elisa was briefly appeased until she noticed the bottle of acetone. The elevator doors began to open on the third floor, but Elisa looked at Edward, still concerned but more perplexed. As she exited the elevator, Edward ingeniously blurted out, "Oh, it's to wipe off permanent marker." Elisa managed to produce a raised eyebrow of satisfaction at that response just before the doors closed, and Edward was on his way to the fourth floor. He was on the verge of buckling under the weight of the day and yet buoyantly anticipating tomorrow because he knew there was no chance it could be as unlucky as today.

Tomorrow it was back to work, where everything was ordinary and predictable. It's not to say Edward was unadventurous or lacking in spontaneity, nor did he have qualms about such things; it was just that his mediocre yet content existence seemed to require that he maintain standards of colouring within the lines. For, as he was taught today, deviation from this norm resulted in what he would have thought was an implausible negative eventuality. Yet, it happened. Arriving at work with a black eye would most definitely cause some concern, and a part of him was surprised to find out he was rather looking forward to the attention.

CHAPTER TWO

Edward manoeuvred his way to the back corner of the sleek silver elevator at Umonoteq, which was crammed to typical 8:37 a.m. capacity. He received only the occasional glance from fellow riders, lasting a mere half-second-longer than usual, at Edward's eye, now a polychromatic range of maroon to yellow. It could have been attributed to the fact that nobody on the way up knew him and therefore couldn't care less about his condition.

As the floor numbers increased, there was more breathing room until eventually, Edward was the solitary occupant reaching his destination: the 27th floor. For a moment, he considered behaving out of character, inventing some extravagant tale about what happened, but he lacked the gregariousness for such a demonstration.

The doors opened, and Edward exited as he usually would, with the same pace, the same intentions, and yet, he felt like he *should* behave differently. He had never been in a fight before, not even as a victim of bullying or a mugging. Not even in elementary school had he fought or participated in wrestling in gym class. Having gone through this many years of his life unscathed in so far as to avoid physical beatings entirely, it *was* something different.

But he didn't know how to behave differently, except that behaving as he was now was different. It was remarkable that he had made it 31-years without even getting punched. This realization was suddenly cut short when Judy, the first of his co-workers, took notice of him.

Not to say that she was his least favourite person, but despite her tiny frame, and nerdy facade, she was the intimidating "cool kid" that he just didn't know how to handle. She always had the wryest of witty comebacks, never cared if you cared, was a loner who was never alone, and was well respected among her co-workers because she excelled in her field. She was as savvy with the abstract as she was with the tech they developed, and for all Edward knew, she had plans to take over the world someday. Her frizzy, ebony ponytails and high school-inspired attire was indeed a clever disguise.

"Jesus, Eddie." She swivelled in her chair to face him. Her excessively large red glasses touched her cheeks when she spoke. She surveyed him with an expression halfway between disgust and pleasure.

"Edward." Edward corrected her for the 817th time.

"Yeah. What happened to your face? Did you get mugged?" Judy leaned back in her chair and crossed her legs, exposing her bare knee through her ripped jeans. She reminded him of a therapist, not offering any sympathy or solution but formulating a biased opinion, waiting for him to disclose all the unspeakable details of last night's incident.

However, Edward continued shuffling past her cubicle with his long stride and, when he was almost out of earshot, declared, "It was a fight." He surprised himself with how hurt he sounded. He got to his desk, which was the second to last cubicle of his row, alongside the window. The last cubicle was kept as a backup station, so no one was hardly ever there. Edward hung up his coat on the cubicle wall and gently slid his backpack under the end of the desk. Judy was suddenly right beside him and Edward hoped that she hadn't noticed him jump.

Judy, with her voice both sharp in tone and intent, tried to whisper and began the crossed-arm interrogation, "A fight? What do you mean, 'a fight'?" If you looked closely, you could see her pupils dilating with arousal, while the rest of her body language had "Whatever" written all over it.

With a modest degree of self-importance, Edward sat down in his swivel chair, raised his right ankle to his left knee, elbows perched on the armrests, tenting his fingertips against each other under his chin. He was now closer to being eye-to-eye with her. "Yeah." There was a significant pause, and just as she was about to press further, Edward whispered, "Suffice it to say, it happened at a Hallowe'en party— but, I'd rather not talk about it."

Judy's dark eyes burned through him like a pair of death rays as if to penetrate his brain for clues, but Edward held on, barely flinching. They stared at each other for a few more seconds. Then Judy broke. She blinked and swiftly gave way to, "Ok, cool. Fair enough," and walked away.

Edward let out a deep, cleansing sigh as he turned to face his desk and start up his computer. He didn't know why Judy always rattled him so, but she did. Logically, it didn't make sense; she wasn't rude or demeaning to him. Nevertheless, he felt like she was the mastermind of the department, possessing tech skills that he could never amass in several lifetimes. She was a wiz-kid, a savant, and he and everyone else on the floor were just simpletons, by comparison, fumbling around with what they learned in university or technical college.

As his computer went through the various start-up protocols, asking for passwords periodically, Edward began to overanalyze Judy's statement. "Cool?" he thought to himself. "OK, cool." Did that mean she thought he was cool because he had been in a fight? No, Edward decided; Judy just wasn't the type to think fighting was cool at all. She must have meant that it was cool if he didn't want to talk about it. Yes, that would be a logical reaction.

And yet, Edward had taken note of her pupils dilating. Although Edward rarely gave himself enough credit for anything, he was remarkably astute in many ways. Unfortunately, he habitually would refrain from sharing his insights with anyone other than Sparky, so he never got the acknowledgment he deserved and subsequently had low confidence in himself.

Being a good 30 cm taller than the cubicle walls, Edward stood up to take an unsuspecting look at Judy, just as his computer loaded its final screen. Despite Judy's desk occupying the first position in front of the elevator, she was already staring directly at him! Quickly, Edward dropped into his chair. His heart was pounding with embarrassment, and he cursed himself for looking like an idiot once again. He concluded that it was entirely plausible that Judy might be a sadist. Potentially, she took pleasure in Edward's beating. Being a vastly superior cerebral creature intellectually, academically, and technologically, Judy, however, lacked size, strength, and physical force. Consequently, she perhaps took delight in the brutal clobbering of this mere mortal.

Before letting the thoughts about Judy's true identity consume him, Edward's strong work ethic kicked back in, and he focused on the tasks at hand. Edward had never missed a day of work, even if he had a cold or flu. Thanks to the location of his cubicle, he could fill himself up with tea and soup all day while coughing and blowing his nose without interfering with anyone else. He wasn't allowed to access the company's mainframe from home due to the proprietary aspect of Umonoteq's apps and gizmos. Still, he was equally happy to come to work every day, even for the minimal human interaction on the bus and at lunchtime.

The buzz of equipment, the occasional telephone ringing, muddled conversation, and barely audible muzak kept Edward on track. At 9:01, the static infused sprinting of Daniel's basketball shoes was heard cornering the first cubicle of the row. As he got closer, the shuffling faded to the spastic rhythm of his breathing. Daniel occupied the cubicle just before Edward's and, for lack of a more endearing term, was Edward's best friend. He tried arduously to be trendy, appealing, likeable, even loveable, and charming. His desperation was often mistaken for insincerity, but none of this bothered Edward. Daniel always had his back. Well, except for last night, of course.

Daniel was too self-absorbed to notice anything else around him as he tried to make it appear that he wasn't almost late. Edward was already deep into his coding to pay much attention to Daniel either.

Peeking around the cubicle wall, Daniel refastened an elastic tie around his 'man-bun,' which wasn't a bun at all, just that his hair was so thick and curly that when pulled back, it looked more like a pompom or rabbit's tail. "Pssst!" he whispered urgently at Edward's back, "was anyone looking for me?" Without looking up or slowing down, the keyboard taps and clicks, Edward blandly replied, "Umm nope." He was intensely focused on what he was doing.

Pleased that no one was enquiring after him but somewhat disappointed that Edward was already knee-deep into his code and wouldn't chat. Daniel tried again, "What are we working on?"

Pausing between clicks, Edward realized he needed to dedicate a little more of Broca's region of his brain to this dialogue; as it's responsible for speaking and writing, he couldn't maintain quality control in both. Without looking away from his screen, Edward, still somewhat monotone, elaborated, "We're still on the Butterfield site's back-end stuff because they didn't give us the mock-up for the interface that we need to do the app yet. So we might as well finish this up, then the ball is in their court." Typing resumed at full speed.

Daniel was satisfied with Edward's logic-driven outline for their next three hours of work and proceeded to stretch, sigh, yawn, and crack his knuckles before delving in himself. Edward just kept on typing. Occasionally he would stop to twist his neck or run his fingers through his hair but otherwise kept going straight to lunch break.

As Daniel's stomach was hardwired to mealtimes, Edward always waited for Daniel's signal. "Dude, that's it, I'm starving. Let's go eat," Daniel announced with a triumphant stretch. The rest of the department was also stirring, as they all usually went to lunch around the same time.

Edward typed his last line of code and quietly exclaimed, "Finished! Where you at?" He stood up and grabbed his coat, waiting for Daniel to emerge from his digital cave. Daniel already had his tweed blazer on and was fastening up the last button when he saw Edward's face for the first time.

"Oh my fucking, god! Dude, your face! What the hell?" He got very close to Edward, grabbed him by both arms as he peered up into his eyes, "Uh, your eye is all..." he recoiled, searching for the best way to describe it while his expression said it all. He looked like he was about to vomit but continued when he found the correct descriptor, "Goopy - like with pus or something."

Edward had forgotten about the beating, mostly on purpose, and was demonstratively punctured by Daniel's look of disgust and went to wipe his eye. "Don't!" Horrified and overdramatic, Daniel slapped Edward's hand away, somehow instinctively channelling his Jewish mother. "Don't touch it! It's full of pus!" The gruesome argument attracted the attention of a few co-workers in the distance.

Trying to deflect the attention, Edward hunched down and whispered, "Ok! Let me get a tissue," as he reached for one on his desk. He carefully wiped his eye, still hiding from the world beyond the cubicle. Daniel went on, "Your eye's so infected; it's black and blue!" He was utterly clueless.

Edward stood up straight and motioned to Daniel to start walking while he muttered under his breath, "It's not infected–" he began to explain, but Daniel cut him off, "It IS SO infected!" But Edward refrained from letting his annoyance get the better of him while he continued to dab his eye with the tissue. "OK, it might be infected, *now*— but I got the black eye *first*." They reached the elevator doors. Most people had already left, so only an older woman from a different department waited behind them. She didn't pay any attention to them at first.

Daniel whispered loudly and impatiently with his teeth somewhat clenched so the woman wouldn't hear him, "You got a black eye? What the hell? How did you get a black eye? Did you get mugged; did you get into a fight?" Edward couldn't get a word in edgewise. He just let Daniel ask and answer his own questions, which could have been entertaining, were it not so exhausting.

As if reading the answers on Edward's face, Daniel gasped, "Whoa, dude, you got into a *fight*?" "*You* got into a fight?" Edward attempted to open his mouth, preparing to provide the details, when the elevator dinged, and Daniel's cell phone rang simultaneously. The elevator doors opened, the three of them entered, and Daniel started speaking in a very different and forced tone.

In an attempt at enthusiasm, Daniel answered, "Hi, *Mom*," he winced as he looked at Edward apologetically. Edward silently mouthed the words, "Don't tell her about this," as he pointed to his face.

Daniel continued with his mother, "What? Nothing's *wrong*. I don't sound *weird*." He shrugged and shook his head, confused and amazed at his mother's ability to read his emotional status in her voice. "Ma, listen— we're in the elevator, heading out for lunch, and you're gonna get cut off s–" She cut him off to ask a question, to which Daniel replied, "Yes, Edward and I, uh-huh, oh he's *fine*." Daniel glared at Edward as the older lady with them suddenly became intrigued by their conversation.

The elevator stopped at the 19th floor to let more people on, at which point Daniel pretended he lost the connection. "Ma, Ma, I gotta go— losing connection— bye," and with that, he hung up on her intentionally. Edward, Daniel, and everyone else politely stared straight ahead as the elevator filled up. Daniel was distressed by having hung up on his mother because he felt like somehow she knew he was just getting rid of her.

"You're probably going to hell for that." Edward scoffed dryly. Several people had squeezed between them. Daniel, still looking forward, quietly confessed, "I know. I know. This is my lot in life. Daniel means 'judged by God'" he shrugged and continued to gesture in despair. Edward was satisfied by the reprieve Daniel's 'mother issues' had provided him.

To Edward's pleasure, Daniel remained utterly silent until the elevator reached the main floor. Everyone exited. As Edward and Daniel came together once again through the lobby, while the crowd dispersed, it was fortunate for Edward that Daniel's self-engrossment led the way.

Daniel held the door for Edward as they headed out for the midday hunting ritual. "I have six sisters, Edward." Edward nodded. He had known Edward since high school, but Daniel continued anyway, "Six sisters, all older than me. And they complain. *They* complain? They're girls; mom and dad wanted a boy, 'just one boy at least' and so they were just girls, and finally this boy comes along, and they're chopped liver. This is all I heard my whole life."

Edward politely nodded as he steered Daniel toward the food truck he preferred. Daniel went along with the lunchtime herd compliantly.

But apparently, Daniel had a point to make, so Edward left the valve open, allowing Daniel to flow at full force. Daniel fervently continued, "So imagine this *boy* who will never be a Jewish doctor. Which is fine because he's got two *sisters* who *are* doctors!" Realizing he had detoured quite majorly from Edward's plight, he then pointed out, "One of which you should see by the way."

Edward moved forward in the food truck line and remarked, "Isn't it 'one of whom'? Anyway, which sister would you recommend; the radiologist or the gynaecologist?" It amused Edward and kept Daniel off-topic.

Daniel dismissed Edward's flippant remarks. "Whatever! So my sisters both marry other Jewish doctors, who are offensively handsome, but one's a plastic surgeon, so who knows, right?"

"Sure," agreed Edward, eager to move the story along.

"Then, what do my parents do? They insist I get a Master's degree, spend another fifty grand, and meanwhile, you're an only child with a bachelor's degree, and you get a job right out of school at Umonoteq. Then I come out *four years later* and sit right next to— who? You!!"

Edward wasn't sure if he should be insulted by that statement because if Daniel was getting to a point, that better not have been it.

The couple ahead had stepped aside, and Edward moved up and asked for a cheeseburger with bacon. Daniel piped in and asked for the same and indicated that he'd pay for both.

Edward bemused, "Hanging up on your mother *and* bacon all in one day?" Daniel waved his hand at him as if erasing a chalkboard. "Never-mind. Back to me sitting next to you. So I'm there, fifty grand more in debt and four years less seniority."

Edward imbued logic wherever he could as a way of diffusing the escalating emotions, "Your parents paid for it, in cash," and then he took his burger from the man in the truck. His "Thanks" was directed at both the man and Daniel.

Daniel insisted, "OK, but I'm indebted to my parents, regardless, and I'm not a doctor, and then my mom wants me to marry a nice Jewish girl and calls me with these antennae-" Edward had to interrupt because he was now sure that there was no point to Daniel's rant. He managed to devour enough of his burger to utter clearly, "Your point?"

"My point?" Daniel exclaimed as he opened the foil paper of his burger, verified that there was indeed bacon under the bun, and continued quieter, "My point is - I love bacon" he took a bite of the burger and continued in the mild ecstasy of the bacon-endorphin reaction, "my sisters think they had it bad, but I'm the one with all the pressure on me, *and* I can't hide anything."

Edward agreed while voraciously consuming the burger, his bruising not interfering as much as he had thought, "Yeah, you're an open book. That's why people like you." Edward was still unsure what Daniel's point was and was now actually open to telling him what happened.

Half knowing the answer, Edward asked, "Why did you hang up on your mother in the first place?" He took another huge bite of his burger as he casually glanced at Daniel as if to say, "My mouth is full, so you'll have to do the talking for this stretch of sidewalk."

Daniel stopped in his tracks and turned squarely to face Edward, gulped down half of what he had in his mouth, and slurped through his next sentence like a feral dog, "Because, I wanted to know what the hell happened to you!" Somehow making the delay sound like it was Edward's fault.

They approached the entrance to Umonoteq, Edward still chewing, with eyes lowered, said, "Well, it's pretty embarrassing, really." Daniel was itchingly eager to know all the embarrassing details. Edward added, "Humiliating." Daniel held the door open again, Edward walked through. He surveyed the lobby to make sure nobody would hear this, but Daniel was still strung up on "humiliating." It was fascinating to him that anyone could lead a more excruciating life than his own, even if it were for only one night every 31 years. "Go on, go on."

They stood in front of the elevator. Edward, carefully wiping his mouth with the burger napkin, reached for the 'up' button with his other hand, exposing another bloody scar. Daniel appraised the gash from a distance. He was impressed. Unlike Edward, he had been beaten up countless times in his youth but never as an adult.

Quickly, people started to congregate at the elevators. There were four elevators on each side of the hallway. Edward looked over at Daniel as if to say it was getting too populated to recount this cringe-worthy tale, but Daniel blurted out, "Ew dude, your eye's all gross again," which made a few people turn around to look then swiftly look away. Edward tried to shush him, but Daniel persisted as he did. "No, seriously; even your eyeball is bloody looking. It's making my eyes water just looking at it."

Edward couldn't shut him up. "Ok, all right. Let's just get on the elevator and go back to work." Daniel was like a child trying to test himself with how much disgust he could tolerate; he just couldn't help staring at Edward's eye. Meanwhile, everyone else was doing their best to avoid eye contact at all costs. The elevator doors opened, and everyone got in.

Daniel simply couldn't leave it alone, and he whispered to Edward, "Did you bust your knuckles from punching one of them?" Others in close proximity were made somewhat uncomfortable by the question and looked disapprovingly at Edward. Mortified, he hid his hands in his pockets and whispered out the side of his mouth, "No–" Daniel leaned in with his right ear, almost elongating his neck so he could be inconspicuously closer. "I think I cut it along some concrete," Edward carried on.

Daniel cringed and buckled slightly as if he had received an injury to his nether regions.

A young woman overheard this and stepped aside apprehensively. Everyone was suddenly giving Edward and Daniel awkward gazes. Without further discussion, they both decided to stay quiet for the rest of the ride or at least until everyone else had exited.

Everyone had cleared out by the 22nd floor. Daniel began prefacing with what he already knew, "OK, let's start from the beginning. You went to the Hallowe'en party."

"Yes." Edward concisely replied as if anticipating a structured list of questions organized like much of the data they deal with daily.

"You went alone?"

"Yep."

"Of course," Daniel knew Edward's real-life friend inventory was sparse. The elevator approached the 24th floor. He persisted, "costume?"

"Yep." Edward managed to get the entire word out in one pitiful breath when Judy got into the elevator, much to their surprise.

Once again, Edward, rattled by her presence, stayed silent and moved aside, refraining from any eye contact. But Daniel, who often spoke before thoughts were formulated, instantly asked, "Where are *you* coming from?" Judy leaned up against the side nearest to Edward. She shrugged one shoulder as she pressed the 'close-door' button. "They have much nicer bathrooms on the 24th," she replied in her usual direct way and added, "but keep it to yourselves; I don't want everyone to know." This information was of little importance to them and consequently was an order they would easily abide by.

Daniel had clued in enough not to persist with questioning Edward while Judy was there. They approached the 27th floor in almost total silence when Judy asked, "Where'd you and Eddie go?". And while Daniel mumbled disinterestedly, "lunch truck" while plucking lint off his sleeve, Edward fumbled forth a reticent, "Edward," followed by an awkward throat clear, with his eyes fixed to the door. Judy glanced up at him, still not acknowledging his insistence on the name correction.

It was not Eddie, Ed, Ted, or any other common nickname, but people always assumed they could arbitrarily alter Edward's name. It slowly unhinged him, forever squeaking in his head like an unoiled gate. He wasn't the type that readily confronted people, yet he never failed to mention the correct version of his name. Regularly, people barely took notice until he corrected them a couple of times, and then they'd usually apologize and make an effort to use the full name. However, Judy was a particular case, as she had never called him Edward, not even when they were first introduced.

It might have been her way of showing how friendly she was or encouraging a cordial atmosphere. Most people would probably warm up to that strategy. Still, Edward interpreted Judy's nicknaming as a way of passive-aggressively undermining him while simultaneously asserting herself as the alpha-brain in the department. His assessment could very well be accurate, for Edward had a difficult time asserting _himself_. Secretly, as much as he tried to avoid Judy altogether, he also tried, in his own suppressed and diligent way, to win the _battle of the nickname_ with her. Most people would call it petty or insignificant, but for Edward, it was a tender blister on the heel of his identity.

The trio exited the elevator on their floor, leaving the empty box to head back downward. Judy robotically arrived at her station while the other two walked around to their side of the room. Co-workers were shuffling around to their places to begin the descent of their day.

As Daniel settled into his cubicle, he noticed Edward was attempting to do the same. Stunned by his audacious stubbornness, he promptly leaned backward in his swivel chair, "What the hell?!" Edward, genuinely startled, replied, "What?"

"Call the freakin' clinic, dude!"

"It's a 'walk-in' clinic. I was just going to go on my way home." Edward's attention had returned to his computer, making his speech less exuberant.

Frustrated, Daniel persisted, "Just make an appointment for 5 pm and leave fifteen minutes early to get there on time."

"It's literally two minutes away," Edward replied.

Daniel swivelled over to Edward's cubicle, "I'm just looking out for you. Trust me; it's easier if you make an appointment. Nobody's going to care if you leave fifteen minutes early with the state you're in."

Edward stopped what he was doing to look over at Daniel. "Fine. Is there a doctor you'd recommend, or you just get whoever is on-call?" Daniel explained, "You get whoever is on-call, unless you go to the hospital, then you might get my sister. Not that I recommend her, but — " Edward cut him off to avoid getting into another conversation about the doctors in Daniel's family. "Ok, ok, I'll call the clinic."

Edward pulled out his phone to search the clinic's website when he realized that Daniel was still sitting there watching. "Can I help you?" sarcastically, Edward asked Daniel, which snapped Daniel back to reality, "no, sorry, I'll get back to work here," and swivelled away to his desk.

Upon finding the phone number and hours of operation, Edward dialled the clinic from his cell phone. He rehearsed his question in his head a few times before someone answered. He uttered his request for an appointment in a firm but quiet voice, "Yes, I'd like to make an appointment for today after five, if possible." The receptionist promptly asked if he could hold. Edward didn't have a chance to reply before the loud and staticky muzak started.

After waiting a few minutes, Edward resumed coding and soon became wholly engrossed in his work that he forgot that he was on hold altogether. After almost ten minutes, the receptionist returned to the line, "You're still holding for whom?" Startled and having to switch his focus, Edward responded with a less than astute sounding, "Uhhhh... nobody."

"Nobody?" replied the receptionist, confused, and who probably misplaced Edward in the queue.

"I mean, I just wanted to make an appointment for today after work because–" Edward managed to regain his focus but was interrupted.

"What time?" This woman was all business.

"Five?" Economizing his words, he put forth a request, with his ductile personality dribbling through the phone.

"No, we're all booked. We're not taking any appointments after 4:30 today."

"What about earlier?" Edward reasoned.

"Booked."

"Ok..." Confused, Edward suddenly realized they were not operating on the same planes of logic, but the receptionist continued.

"Is it an emergency?" sounding hopeful.

Edward tried to be assertive, "Well, yes, in a way, I guess, I do need to have it looked at today."

The receptionist concluded, "OK, then you need to go to the emergency room at the hospital."

Deflated by the futility of this exercise, Edward conceded, "OK, thanks," while inside, he heard himself want to say, "thanks for nothing." She promptly hung up on him.

This was not unlike most conversations Edward had with strangers on the phone, customer service reps, or even when ordering take-out. He was always shy and unassertive, shrinking into a dwarfish shadow of himself. He was all too often like a starving peasant kneeling at the foot of the gatekeeper— even if that was a lowly gatekeeper taking his pizza order. He no longer harboured feelings of embarrassment regarding the matter and just accepted the fact that these types of situations caused him a great deal of anxiety.

Edward rejoined reality and leaned back in his chair, "Daniel?" He whispered. Daniel leaned back from his cubicle with a head nod. Edward reported, "The clinic's booked, so she said I have to go to the emerge. Do you really think I need to see a doctor?"

Daniel, well versed in the guilt-tripping mechanism, nonchalantly and passive-aggressively said, "Yes, I do. But do what you want. Your eye is definitely infected though, dude." and he swivelled back to his usual position.

Edward let out a big frustrated, dramatic sigh. "Fine. But I'm not going until the end of the day. I'll probably have to wait for hours anyway." There was a part of him that secretly hoped everything would miraculously clear up on its own.

The day went on, and Edward was typically productive with all the new tasks set out for him. He hadn't budged from his seat and only looked away from his computer occasionally to reach his water bottle. He had almost forgotten about going to the doctor when Daniel suddenly appeared beside him getting his coat on.

"I'll walk with you. Maybe my sister's there." Daniel stood waiting while Edward logged out of everything. One window after the next went black and powered down. Outside, it was already dusk. It seemed as if Daniel didn't fully trust that Edward would go to the hospital on his own and waited patiently while Edward went through his routine.

The two walked towards the elevator, and Edward braced himself as he turned the corner for his regular end-of-the-day encounter with Judy. However, she wasn't there, and Edward was surprised at how relieved he was that he didn't have to interact with her.

Daniel was unusually quiet, riveted by the information on his phone. They got in the elevator and began their descent. About halfway down, Daniel stopped texting and put his phone in his pocket. He appeared to return to normal, "Bummer, my sister's not on tonight, and she's not sure who is." alluding to the fact that she could have possibly reduced Edward's wait-time.

"No, that's fine; I don't mind waiting." Edward really didn't have a choice at this point. His eye was not improving. After the beating he took, he was grateful that all he had to deal with was some unsightly bruising and a goopy eye. As if plucking the thought from Edward's mind, Daniel recalled, "You still didn't tell me what happened." Edward wasn't in the mood to get into it. The crowd of people trying to put their workday behind them as if pushing and rushing to save a few seconds would make a noticeable difference in anyone's life.

Daniel and Edward made their way out of the building as it just started to drizzle. Edward asked as he noticed Daniel was coming along with him, "Didn't you drive your car today?"

"Yeah, but I have nothing to do right away. I figured I'd hang out with you for a bit. Besides, I need to hear what happened." Daniel stammered with the chill as he tried to cover up.

Edward began to formulate his thoughts. "All right, so I went to the party alone, which is, you know—"

Daniel piped in, "Yeah, uncharacteristic, to say the least."

"Exactly." Edward agreed and continued. "So that was odd for me, but fine at the same time, for some reason. It was an ok location; everyone was in costume, and maybe 50% full."

Daniel was picturing it. "But what was your costume? You didn't say." Just then, Daniel's mobile rang, and he stopped walking to answer it.

"Hey." He answered and paused. The voice on the phoned sounded female and agitated.

"What?" Daniel sounded surprised. "Shit. I totally forgot. OK, I'll go right now." and hung up.

Edward concerned, "What's wrong?" Daniel already started to turn back. "I promised my mom that I'd be there to help when my dad started with the plumbing in the basement because he'll wreck it." It didn't matter to Edward, but he shrugged and offered his opinion, "You don't know anything about plumbing either." Daniel was rushing away and called back, "I know! I'm supposed to be there to insist that he call a plumber!" and with that, he turned and trotted back towards work, where he had left his car in the underground employee parking.

Edward was again mildly relieved. He would be able to sit and wait in peace once he got there. Edward loved Daniel like a brother, but unless he was working, Daniel felt that prolonged silence was awkward and something to be remedied. Even when complaining, he was always entertaining, but he had no "off-switch." Then there was still the issue of the party and the fight. In truth, Edward would have preferred to never speak of it again. Call it a blip in the program, or a lump in the pancake batter, albeit it caused a great deal more discomfort than either of those things and even to call it discomfort was trivializing it!

Hustling along the sidewalk, Edward was still exchanging odd glances with the passersby as the icy drizzle stung his face. He could see the red and white light of the emergency entrance to the hospital, and as he approached, the sidewalk was cluttered with patients smoking. They maintained their twenty-meter distance obediently; two were in wheelchairs, and one was out in his shoes, hospital gown and IV pole. Edward felt like they were three portends of what the night had in store for him. Unlike the sirens, luring and attractive, they were more like living gargoyles warning of his fate once he crossed the threshold.

"It's now or never," Edward thought to himself while he averted his gaze as he passed the smokers and committed himself to enter the building. Inside, he made a cursory assessment of his surroundings and proceeded to the admissions queue. Once seated, there would be enough time to take in each and every peculiar patient.

As he stood in the short line, trying not to listen to the ailments of the man at the window, he questioned himself. Within himself, as far out as he could see, looking out his own eyes, at the view, at the parts of him that he could see, he was normal. He had a clean overcoat, grey tweed of considerable quality, heavy shoes which were a recent purchase, work casual trousers, a bland wool scarf, and a faux-leather satchel. Everyone else there was peculiar.

But Edward began to imagine what the peculiar people must have thought when they looked at him. He turned slightly and caught a glimpse of himself as a faint reflection in the glass. The poor fluorescent lighting overhead greatly accentuated his scars and shadows, and he looked far from soft, gentle, or shy. He almost looked menacing if anyone cared to label him.

The queue moved up. The next character at the window was a young man almost as tall as Edward, possibly close to his age. It was difficult to tell, as the fellow was affected by some form of addiction. He was wearing a silky, purple nylon tracksuit, and shiny white Nikes. The entire ensemble was brand new, and the suit still had crease marks in it from being packaged. In a loud intelligible voice, the guy asked, "I just need a new sling for my arm." The triage nurse looked at him and smiled kindly while she responded. Edward couldn't make out what she said, but the guy explained further, "Yeah, I was here the other day, and I woke up just now, and someone had stolen my sling."

Edward found it ironic. Here was a young man, in what Edward presumed was a freshly stolen outfit which wasn't much of a disguise as it still screamed, "douchebag." Moreover, he couldn't help notice how polite and extraverted the guy was. He could have worked in sales, in a different time or place, and for all Edward knew, he was an entrepreneur of sorts just dealing with products of a more illicit nature.

In some ways, Edward felt ashamed. Not for calling the guy a douchebag because he wore a purple tracksuit, but for the fact that even that guy was more outgoing than him. He was assertive, polite, and forward, even if he was potentially a criminal. On the other hand, Edward was introverted, unnecessarily timid, and not to mention backward. "Backward," a word his father often called him in frustration.

Next up was the rotund misshapen lady with a cane just in front of Edward. Mr.Purple had moved aside to wait for his sling. Edward made sure his toes were behind the peeling red tape on the floor. "Please stand behind this line," a little sign said, in a sweet and kind voice, he imagined. Obediently, Edward waited. This was just the beginning of a long night's tournament of "who has the most urgent ailment." Edward knew he couldn't win at that game. He would sit quietly in an attempt to avoid bizarre conversations with lunatics and keep from touching anything so as not to become infected with necrotizing fasciitis.

Edward could not overhear the entire conversation between the woman ahead of him and the nurse behind the glass, but he could hear the tone. The patient sounded as if she made frequent visits to the hospital as Edward managed to pick out words like "usual," "last time," and "Dr. Wilkins said." The nurse also seemed familiar with her and surprisingly unimpressed with her story compared to her reaction to the young man who preceded her.

The woman seemed to want to keep talking, but the nurse was trying to get her to move along; she had all the information she needed and kept attempting to have the woman sit down. Finally, she succeeded and let out a big sigh as the woman moved away from the window, ever so cumbersomely.

Edward stepped to the window and began describing his condition. Perhaps it was because the nurse was still frustrated by the previous patient, but she sharply interjected, "Could you speak up, I can't understand a word you're saying." Edward leaned into the glass as much as possible, slouching toward the metal slats through which the sound travelled best. He cleared his throat as if preparing to deliver a momentous speech but spoke only slightly louder than the first time. "I have an infected eyeball." He opted for the short version this time, but wondered to himself, why he had said 'eyeball' rather than just 'eye' and began to feel a warm wave of embarrassment roll up his face.

The nurse, of course, made it worse, "Eye*ball*?" she blurted out. "Uh, yes, um, my eye, actually. It's, it *seems* to be infected, by some— thing." Edward was drowning. The nurse glared at him as if he was an imbecile. Edward could offer nothing else but pointed to the goopy eye while smiling pitifully.

"Healthcare card," the nurse demanded as she broke the stare. Edward slipped his card in the germ-laden tray slot, and the nurse entered the numbers into the computer and slipped it back to him. "Have a seat. It'll be a while." and she swivelled away.

Relieved to some degree that the introduction was over, Edward scanned the room for the best possible location. He had to be strategic in his planning, not near the draughty entrance, not near the weirdos, not trapped or cornered, with a good view of where the doctors might come in from and not with anyone behind him. He could have opted for a view of the television, but those spots were taken by a woman and her mucous oozing child, a middle-aged man who coughed with his mouth open, a teenage boy with an ice-pack on his ankle and his dad, presumably.

Finally, Edward spotted the ideal seat; it was at the end of the row towards the back wall, closest to where he'd most likely have to go next. He figured he would be there for a couple of hours at least, so he might as well get it right. Edward valiantly made his way to a seat and set himself up in such a way that he wouldn't have to touch anything. He unbuttoned his coat, made sure his gloves were securely in his pockets, took out his phone and began to check his Facebook.

Moments later, the intake nurse opened the side door presenting a fresh new sling to the man in the shiny purple nylon ensemble. She was all smiles and pleasantries, but not to Edward. The young man jaunted towards the exit, ready to carry on whatever scoundrelly pursuits in which he would typically engage. It baffled Edward. Neither did he look down his nose at him (much), nor did he want to be like him, but he couldn't be like him even if he wanted to.

But Edward *had* gotten into a fight, he thought proudly to himself, and he *was* sporting a black eye— which was now infected. Indeed a short-lived victory. Edward peered into his Facebook and gave the thumbs-up to a variety of posts and the occasional, "Hahaha," followed by a laughing face, for he was adamantly *never* going to prescribe to, "LOL-ing" even if his life depended upon it. Daniel, however, was not so staunch in his convictions, for Edward had even heard him more than once actually say "LOL" aloud instead of laughing. He loved Daniel like a brother, despite that.

CHAPTER THREE

Hours went by. People came and went. Edward saw blood running down someone's leg, a drunk guy vomiting, the police escorting another guy out, the broken ankle teenager had gone, the snotty kid had gone as well. Everyone who was ahead of Edward was gone.

He wanted to find a vending machine to ease his grumbling stomach, but he'd been there too long to be sure that they wouldn't call his name at that moment. As Murphy's Law would dictate, that's *precisely* when they *would* call his name. So he waited. Sleepy and hungry.

Another fifteen minutes had passed. That was it. Edward suddenly stood up, about to venture forth in search of a food-like substance encased in plastic, when a tall, auburn-haired woman in scrubs and glasses appeared by his side. She held a chart in her hand, smiling at Edward and instinctively knowing this was her next patient.

"Edward, I presume?" She had a firm but silky voice that reached out with surprising warmth. She continued to smile cordially. Edward sprang back into the present moment and exclaimed eagerly, "Yes!" He was pleased that his grasp of the inner workings of Murphy's Law resulted favourably this one time.

"Follow me. Let's go take a look at that eye." This also solved the question Edward was pondering, which was with all the people in the waiting room, how did she know it was him. He tended to forget that it was incredibly apparent to anyone looking at him.

Edward followed the woman down the hall to another large room with several curtained-off examination areas. She gestured to him to go into the second section and instructed him further, "You can hang your coat here, and if you wish to disrobe and put on the gown, that's fine too."

Edward stopped in his tracks, hands positioned to lift off his coat, frozen. He stared at her. She continued as if to clarify, "Would you feel more comfortable with the gown for the examination?"

No.

No, Edward would *not* feel more comfortable in the gown. Vulnerable and quite *un*comfortable is what he would feel! But he couldn't say that. She smiled. "You know what, it's fine. We're just looking at the eye. Correct?"

"Yes, just the eye." Edward assured her, as well as himself, and glad that he didn't say, 'eyeball' again.

She left for a moment while Edward had just enough time to hang up his coat and sit on the paper-coated examination table. She returned with a variety of utensils, swabs, gauze, a squirt bottle, and so on.

Not usually great at initiating small talk, Edward quickly asked, "Are you the doctor?"

"No, I'm *the nurse,*" she replied, mimicking Edward's tone while she slapped on a couple of non-latex gloves from the box on the table. "You might not need the doctor."

Edward didn't want her to feel like he was insinuating that his malady required a doctor and started fumbling, "Oh, I just thought you were the doctor because my friend's sister is a doctor here. My best friend."

She started looking into Edward's eye, holding the eyelids apart, when she asked inquisitively, "Oh, what's her name?" and continued to look all around Edward's eye. "Look around in a big circle."

"Rebecca," Edward had to answer questions on an unrelated subject while rotating his eyes in a circular motion, not unlike tapping one's head while rubbing one's stomach.

"Could you lie down for me? I'm going to flush it out, clean up the eye, and then see where we're at," she informed him. Edward twisted himself on the paper, ripped it and then apologized repeatedly. The nurse continued, as she slowly squirted some sterile solution in Edward's eye, "Rebecca?"

Edward corrected himself, "Uh yes, Dr.Hess. Or maybe she goes by Dr.Lehman."

The nurse wiped Edward's eye and flushed it some more. "Ah, yes, Dr.Hess. She's married to Dr. Lehman, isn't she?"

Edward felt strangely relaxed on the table, hands folded humbly across his stomach, and noticed a trickle of water running out his eye. It was soothing. "Yeah, she's married to him, Dr.Lehman."

The nurse continued making sure Edward's eye was immaculate and that there were no tears or cuts anywhere. "So what happened? Did you injure yourself playing sports?" she asked.

Edward let out a nervous giggle, "Sports? Uh, no..." Edward smiled. He was tickled by the fact that she would guess he injured himself playing sports rather than get into a fight. He was flattered, actually.

The nurse stopped, stepped back and looked at Edward rather than his eye. "What's so funny? What happened?"

Edward didn't want her to think he was some kind of ruffian, so he chose his words carefully. "Somebody hit me."

"Hit you?" She sounded very concerned. "Were you mugged?" and she then proceeded to motion to Edward to sit back up.

Edward sat up and looked into his hands, "No, I was at a party."

"A party?"

"Yeah." Edward sighed and tried not to make eye contact.

"Someone you knew?"

"Nope."

"Did you press charges?"

"Nope."

They stared at each other for a few moments. Edward wasn't sure where she was going with this.

"I need to ask you a few questions. Did you sustain any injuries to any other parts of your body? Did you get assaulted anywhere else on your body?"

Edward felt an odd sense of self-importance and humiliation simultaneously. "I scraped my knuckles on concrete," he said as he uncovered his hand. The nurse looked at Edward's hand. It was scraped and scabby but clean. She asked again, "Anywhere else? Blows to the head? Were you hit with an object?" She didn't sound annoyed at all, just very compassionate.

Edward shrugged, "Uh, nowhere, really, just a punch in the face." He raised his eyes to hers finally. She was frowning. "Do you often get in fights?"

"Often? No, never. I don't think this would even be considered a *fight,* seeing as it was pretty one-sided. I didn't exactly *participate*." Edward was being somewhat jovial and free-flowing with his answers, which was very much out of the ordinary. It seemed to put the nurse at ease as well, at least enough to bring her smile back.

"Okay. And you didn't get robbed?" She asked again. Edward shook his head, "nope."

"Nothing else hurts?"

"No, everything is fine; just my pride is a little wounded."

"That'll be easy enough to recover. Give me a moment, and I'll get the doctor to write you a prescription for some antibiotic drops. You don't have any tears; it looks like it was just foreign particles and bacteria causing a problem. If you use the drops right away and then twice a day after that for a week, you should be as good as new. The bruising might still have a few shades to go through before that's all gone."

She took all her utensils away. Edward sat there feeling different. Most people's legs probably dangled from the table, but not his. He felt good, confident even. It was highly irregular. He found himself smiling from the inside out.

A few minutes passed, and he heard two pairs of footsteps approaching. A small-framed, older Indian man with thick, curly grey hair, wearing dark blue scrubs and a stethoscope around his neck, came with the nurse. "Well, well! Hello, I'm Dr.Sivanda. Clotilde tells me you had a nasty eye infection, hmm?"

"Yes," Edward answered firmly. He was too focused on the fact that he had just learned the nurse's name. Clotilde. He had nothing clever to say.

The doctor and Clotilde exchanged glances, and then Dr.Sivanda continued, "All right, I'm just going to give you a prescription for drops. It's important to follow exactly what it says," with each statement, he rhythmically tapped the air with his bony index finger toward Edward, "don't put anything foreign in the eye. Wipe with sterile gauze, clean hands, clean gauze instead of a towel, ok?" He was firm and kind. Then he turned to Clotilde, "Give him extra packets of gauze he can use."

"OK," obliged Clotilde.

The doctor scribbled out a prescription. "There you go, young man. I hope we never meet again!" he let out a big belly laugh and receded behind the outer curtain. Both Edward and Clotilde laughed. "Emerge humour," she said and handed Edward a small stack of gauze packets and the prescription.

Edward stood up, placed the items on the table, and began to get his coat when more small-talk inexplicably took over him. "So what kind of name is Clotilde?" She paused as she was about to walk away, but Edward couldn't see that. Had he, he might not have started speaking.

"French." She said, in a way that sounded like she must get asked that all the time.

Edward got his coat on. "Ah. I guess there's no English equivalent?"

"There is actually, *Clotilda*." She shrugged.

"I never heard of that." Edward confessed as he put the gauze in his pockets, just as Clotilde was simultaneously saying, "You probably never heard - yeah." They chuckled.

There was an awkward moment between them, but Edward had no idea that it was equally uncomfortable for Clotilde. He didn't notice such things, nor even aware that such things were possible for other people. He was the only awkward creature on the entire planet, as far as he knew. Everyone else seemed to know exactly what to do and say at any given moment.

"Well, stay out of trouble, eh?" joked Clotilde. "Yes, I plan on it. Bye. Thank you." Edward fumbled around as he politely walked past her while showing gratitude and maintaining profession- alism. He accidentally kicked the leg of the metal chair, which made an unimaginable loud clanking. He apologized to it a few times under his breath as he made his way around the corner and reintroduced himself to the waiting room, where every pair of eyeballs was on him.

Edward scurried as he did, paying extra attention to his steps so as not to trip, kick something, make another loud noise or injure anyone - at least until he was outside. Gloves on, bracing the chilly air, he thought perhaps he should go to the pharmacy, and in the time it would take to fill the prescription, he could pick up something to eat.

It was almost 9 pm, and he was famished. Sparky had an automatic feeder, but despite that, he knew that he would start to get antsy having been alone for so long. However, on the upside, his eye felt greatly improved just by having had it cleaned up by Clotilde.

And then there was Clotilde.

CHAPTER FOUR

Once Edward's eye cleared up, and the bruising would be gone, then perhaps people would stop asking him what happened, and he would be able to pretend the incident never happened at all.

The streets were more populated than last night, probably because it was a Thursday and still early. Edward dashed as speedily as he could to the drugstore. He knew this visit would be significantly better than the last one. There was no nail polish remover to buy, most likely fewer strange characters, more regular people doing regular shopping, and he could just go in and get his eyedrops and be done with it.

If he timed everything right, he could coordinate his take-out food to be delivered shortly after he reached home. After the last 24 hours, which were excruciating, Edward felt that he could justify ordering multiple dishes from the Szechuan place rather than settle for "meal #3 for two". If his pain and misery weren't enough justification, he also decided that he could take the leftovers to work tomorrow for lunch and possibly have some for tomorrow's supper too. Edward wasn't cheap, but he was frugal.

Whenever he decided to splurge on something for himself, there was always a lengthy inner presentation of all the reasons why it was not only a justified action, but it made the most sense. As a result of the decision, it ultimately improved his life in numerous ways. It was always the same procedure.

Edward lived alone, saved money, worked consistently, had no bad habits, budgeted more or less, paid all his bills on time, and even managed to save a little every month. He had no one to answer to, and he was an unusually responsible person by all accounts. He reassured himself that a less unusual person would probably have saved less, partied more, and definitely gotten into more fights.

Edward skipped onto the curb at the drugstore entrance, as he did now, and he wondered about how Daniel was faring at his parent's house. There was always a great deal of drama in Daniel's life, but it was more about Daniel's reaction to things than the existence of things to react to.

At the back of the drugstore, it seemed much quieter. Many people were shopping, but no one else was getting prescriptions. Edward stood under the sign that said, "Drop off prescriptions here." He saw the tiny Asian pharmacist scurry back and forth, muttering to herself and placing packets and pill bottles in little compartments. Uncharacteristically, he said, "Um, excuse me," trying to get her attention.

Without looking up, she chimed back politely and breathlessly, "I'll be with you in a second. I'm so busy. I'm here all alone!" Edward felt that he was missing something. He looked around again. He was still the only one there. Unless a considerable number of people had just dropped off prescriptions at the same time prior to his arrival and then suddenly vanished, he couldn't understand what she was on about.

Sensing Edward's confusion, she finally stopped her scurrying and took a nice deep breath, "I know it looks like you're the only one here, but we get most of the scripts as refills and people just call them in, and we deliver. I had two pharmacists cancel tonight." She adjusted her glasses and smiled up at Edward despite being on a raised platform.

"Ahh, I understand," said Edward, feeling bad that he initially thought she had fed him an excuse. He handed her the prescription, "I need to get these drops. Will it take long?" he gave her his best passive anxious look, unintentionally, of course.

"Uh, oh yeah. I'll give you this one right away. Are you in the system?" She took it to the computer. "Yes, I must be," responded Edward brightly.

"Yes, yes, here you are. OK, last time you had a sinus infection. That's a long time ago! Good for you." She laughed. Edward laughed and stepped aside from the drop-off location.

Edward reached into his pocket, took out his phone and looked up the Szechuan place. He dialled.

"'Ello?"

"Yes, hi, could I order for delivery?"

"Ya, go 'head."

"Could I get the Szechuan chicken, spicy, the fried noodles with beef and bok choi, the vegetable fried rice, and the mixed veg with cashews?"

"Dis, Ed?"

"Pardon me?"

"You Ed? From Clairvale?"

"Oh, yes, yes."

"Special occasion? You don't wanna numba free that you always get?"

"Number 3? No, no, not today."

Edward suddenly realized that even other people, including those he had never met in person, thought him to be undeniably predictable. He *did* always order meal number 3 for two people, even though it was always just for himself.

Although he took his predictability to be akin to reliability, at this moment, it was beginning to annoy him. Edward was not aware that he was annoyed yet, because he often kept secrets from himself. For now, his self-annoyance had only just landed at the inbox, in the 'new and uncomfortable feelings' department's front desk. It would take some time to make its way to the top floor CEO of Awareness' office, where he would eventually have to address it.

"Edward?" The pharmacist called to him, and he obediently and promptly ran up to the sign that said, "Pick-up Prescriptions Here." There were still no other clients present. She rustled around with papers and labels, pealing, sticking, stapling, and bagging, which all sounded very important to Edward compared to his work sounds, which were nothing but him typing and clicking and staring at a screen all day. Somehow dispensing pharmaceuticals looked more like real work.

The pharmacist explained what Edward needed to do with the drops and rang it through the cash register. Edward was paying when he received a text from Daniel. He completed his transaction, thanked the woman, and made his way to the exit. He needed to be quick so that he would arrive home before the restaurant delivery did.

Dodging people on the sidewalk, Edward's phone beeped another reminder that he hadn't looked at the text yet.

Daniel: "Dude!! These people are KILLING me!!!!!"

Had it been anyone else, it might have looked like an urgent, or at least an alarming, text. Edward was well aware that Daniel was referring to his parents. They were most likely *not* killing him, but up to their usual shenanigans of either comfort-arguing or hounding Daniel on several unresolved topics, such as marriage, real estate, hairstyles, careers, and general good habits of a thirty-something Jewish son.

There was nothing much to offer in response, and Edward was still rushing, so he simply spoke to text, "My heart bleeds. Running home from pharmacy. Starving!"

Daniel quickly replied, "OMG, So late! Call later." But Edward didn't know if that meant Daniel would call later or if he wanted Edward to call him later. It didn't matter. All Edward wanted was to get home and eat.

Edward briskly opened the door to his apartment, where an irritated Sparky voiced his displeasure. Edward kicked off his shoes, ran around with his coat still on, closed curtains and blinds all to the litany of grievances by Sparky's loud and varied meows. He threw his coat on the sofa, then Edward had to get to the toilet before his bladder exploded and finally was about to pick up Sparky, who was still complaining when the buzzer went off.

This was a sound that always made Sparky run and hide. Running back to the front door, Edward grabbed his wallet from his coat pocket and buzzed the delivery person in. Sparky bravely poked his head out from under the sofa skirt. Edward poised with a hand on the doorknob, waiting to hear the elevator doors open, squinted at Sparky. "You're such a chicken shit. Nothing to say now, eh?"

The elevator bell pinged, and Edward systematically opened his door, debit card at the ready. A muscular girl with bright blue hair fading into blond and sporting several piercings, carrying the debit machine and a large paper bag stapled shut with the bill affixed to it, looked both ways and then saw Edward. It was their first time meeting.

"Hey," she nodded.

"Hey," Edward mirrored. There was no way this girl could mistake Edward for being one of her peers despite his cool attempt and head nod.

"You need the machine?" she asked as she conscientiously handed him the large bag.

"Yep." Edward maintaining his nonchalance, placed the bag down on the floor inside his apartment. The smell of the food lured Sparky out of his hiding place, and he began to purr and nuzzle the folded corner of the crisp paper bag.

As Edward tapped away at the machine, the girl suddenly reverted to a five-year-old version of herself and let out a delighted squeal upon seeing Sparky.

Edward turned with a jerk as the girl continued to invade his space. The machine was spewing paper receipts, but she was suddenly on all fours petting Sparky with the knees of her punk-themed multicoloured leggings sticking to the mat.

"Aww, he's so cute!" She proceeded to pick him up and cuddle Sparky in her arms like a baby. This was not what Edward would consider normal or appropriate, and he found himself frowning awkwardly, holding the debit machine in one hand and his card in the other, shyly offering her the device and mumbling, "hmmm, that's interesting; he doesn't typically like people. I guess he was alone too long today."

The girl paid no attention to Edward and continued nuzzling Sparky, who ruthlessly flaunted his affection for her right under Edward's nose. "Okay, that's enough, Sparky, let the young lady get back to work."

The girl whispered inaudible sweet nothings to Sparky as she gently let him bounce down to the floor. The sheer fickleness of this well-cared-for feline really ruffled Edward's feathers. That would teach him not to leave Sparky alone for so long. It only took a few more hours for him to forget that Edward was his primary caregiver. Now that Sparky's food was provided with a timed dispenser, he didn't look to Edward to fulfill such basic needs.

"Do you want your receipt?" The girl asked politely with a glow on her face. It seemed Sparky's hugs had made her evening. Dryly, "No thanks," Edward replied, and the girl walked away.

Edward closed the door and glared at Sparky, who sat there proudly. "Really?" Sparky knew precisely what he had done.

As soon as Edward had emptied the bag and set out all the containers on the table, ready to serve himself, he received another text. It was too late to postpone eating any further and just ignored the phone. With the pleasurable sensations that accompany a soon-to-be satiated man, Edward raised the volume on the TV remote to drown out his cell phone beeps. The rush of carbs, sweetness, heat, crispness, and gooeyness all contributed to his euphoria. Sparky decided to behave himself and was crunching submissively at his dish.

The plate was scraped completely clean. Edward had started with chopsticks but finished off with a spoon. His hands were sticky, and he had no idea how he managed to get sticky sauce up past his wrist. Once everything was cleared, Edward prepared one large container for his lunch the following day, which was fast approaching.

Sparky, equally satisfied, was already curled up in his after-dinner spot on the sofa. Edward tidied up the kitchen, folded the bag, placed it in the recycling bin, and rewashed his hands before attempting his new eye-cleaning ritual.

Edward proceeded to open the package in the bathroom, which was no easy feat. It involved a towel, teeth, and eventually pliers. He had his clean gauze at the ready to wipe the eye and put exactly two drops in, wiped the eye again. Edward put the tiny bottle into the medicine cabinet. When he closed the door, he examined his face in the mirror of his dimly lit bathroom. The bruising had changed colour. His flawless complexion was now distorted. Anyone who looked at him had a distorted view of him, at least physically.

"Attractive" wasn't a word Edward would have used to describe himself. Rather "bland and inoffensive" or "forgettably plain" would be closer to what he believed about himself. But now, with this chartreuse and purple discolouration, he felt even less than that. What he thought would make most guys more impressive looking made Edward feel worse. He let out a deep sigh, and his thoughts went back to Clotilde. He wondered what she would have thought of him had she met him under different circumstances.

His feelings of accomplishment and satisfaction shifted inexplicably to apathy. He went about his nightly shutdown rituals; he turned off everything in the living room, hung up his coat, emptied his pockets, and realized he hadn't checked his phone. There were six messages from Daniel.

"Dude. Call me!!!!!"

"Are you home?"

"I gotta talk to you."

"NOW. DUDE. CALL ME."

"Are you OK? OK, I'm worried now."

"Edward WTF srly worried now. Did you get into another fight?!?!"

It was precisely what Edward needed to snap out of his funk. Sometimes, Daniel seemed to channel an old Jewish woman, if she spoke in text, of course. It made him smile. Edward was accustomed to Daniel in a way that likened him to the boy who cried wolf. There was no such thing as an emergency in Daniel's life because everything was an emergency, or nothing was going on.

Edward took his time to get ready for bed. He plugged his phone into the charger beside his bed, then put on pyjamas, and then went to brush his teeth. Sparky watched the procedures as he usually did, but he was always especially intrigued by the toothpaste as it was spat into the sink.

Everything was still relatively messy in the bedroom, and Edward decided that he'd thoroughly tidy up on the weekend. He turned off the overhead light and climbed into the bed on the far side where the lamp was still on, and he reached for his phone to text Daniel before calling it a night.

Edward texted: "Got your messages. Was tired, hungry, ate, going to bed now so will talk to you tomorrow." and hit the send button. He hardly had a chance to place the phone back on the nightstand when Daniel called back.

Amused at Daniel's tenacity, Edward, comfortably in bed, reluctantly answered, "What's up?" while still smiling sleepily.

Without so much as a 'hello,' Daniel blurted out, "So what's up with the nurse?!"

Edward's eyes opened again, and his breath quickened. "What?"

Daniel had mastered a way to both shout and whisper simultaneously, "A nurse from the hospital was asking my sister about you."

Edward sprung up to a seated position instantaneously; the mere act extracted the charger from the wall, and it tumbled across the floor. "Clotilde?!" Edward gasped.

Daniel, pleasantly surprised, warmly responded, "Yes...." As if being called to duty, Edward vaulted out of bed, stood up straight, and began to pace back and forth in the newly created bedside trench with the charger dangling from the phone indiscriminately bumping his legs. Daniel continued, "So, are you going to tell me what happened or what?"

Mentally and physically fumbling, Edward responded, "What? *I* don't know anything. *You're* the one with all the info. What was she asking? Was it like medical stuff, or...?"

Daniel enjoyed how flustered Edward was, and they both realized, simultaneously yet separately, that perhaps Edward actually found Clotilde attractive. It was something that didn't happen often. Edward always imagined that if he were ever going to be with a woman again, she'd probably have to make her interest unmistakably apparent, or he would never have the gumption to make the first move.

"*Medical* stuff? Are you *kidding* me? She can't ask my sister that! She's got a mental file on your medical history!" Daniel was not shy to boast his glee resulting from how discombobulated Edward sounded. There was a moment of silence.

"What? Enough with the dramatic pause. What was she asking; just tell me already. I was about to go to sleep, and now— well, I'm wide awake now." Edward blathered, and Daniel chuckled.

Not wanting to prolong the agony unnecessarily, Daniel slowly explained, "She asked my sister if she knew you. She said she did."

"Uh-huh," Edward muttered, breathlessly and still pacing and pausing.

"Then she asked if you had a girlfriend."

"Uh-huh. Yeah, and I don't."

"Exactly, and that's what my sister said. Well - she said, she didn't think so."

"That was kind of her."

"Then she asked if you were gay, and my sister said -"

"What!? Does she think I'm gay?"

"No!"

"Then why is she asking?!" Edward ran his hand up through the crown of his hair and stopped frozen there until Daniel continued.

"No, no, I think she was just making sure."

Edward let out a big sigh and dropped his hand back to his side. "ok, ok, go on."

Daniel continued, "So then she asked if you were normal."

"Jesus!" Edward slapped his forehead.

Daniel started to chuckle, "and my sister said that she told her, *yeah, he's more normal than my brother*, which is lovely to hear, from one's sibling."

"Yeah, yeah, Daniel, this isn't about you." Edward was unanticipatedly impatient. "So what else?"

"Apparently, that was it. They had to go do something. My sister had to go. So that's all I know. But the way my sister said it, she said it sounded like this chick *really took a shine to you*."

Edward flopped back on the bed, excessively rubbed his furrowed forehead, and squished his eyelids tightly together. "What's that supposed to *mean*, though? What am I supposed to *do* with that? I can't ask your *sister* to be the go-between. It's embarrassing!"

"Why is it embarrassing?"

Edward stared wide-eyed at the ceiling. In one short minute, he had flown through the feelings of surprise, lust, infatuation, the wedding, the honeymoon, the divorce, and finally, grief. "Why did you tell me this now? This could have waited until tomorrow."

Daniel, unsympathetic to Edward's woes, ignored his misplaced bundle of emotions and stated, "No, I'm your friend, the bearer of good tidings. This is good. I'll talk to you tomorrow."

"It's awful."

"Goodbye, Edward." Daniel's smile could be heard through the phone, making Edward feel sick to his stomach.

"Ugh."

"Say 'good-bye'"

"Ugh."

"Edward? You're being childish."

"I know. I feel stupid."

"Do you like her?"

"*No*.

I don't know.

Yeah. I suppose.

I mean, she was nice."

"Well, ok then."

"Ok, bye. I'll see you tomorrow."

They both hung up, and Edward dropped his hand toward the floor, still clutching the phone. He had no idea how he was supposed to sleep with this new information. He truly *did* feel stupid. It was something unexpected and yet positive, and he was now embarrassed by his reaction, which made him feel even more foolish.

Edward lay there like he'd been hit with a taser for a moment until Sparky began nesting on the adjacent pillow. Sparky was unamused by all this activity and glared at Edward as if to comment on how ridiculous he thought Edward was behaving.

"Don't mock me." Edward glared back at Sparky and then began putting his phone in place to charge on the nightstand while he mumbled. "Normal? What kind of question is that? I talk to my cat, and I get in fights, ha!" He argued with his covers and mumbled some more until a long boney arm came out to pat Sparky on the head. "'Night, Sparky." and with that, Edward compelled himself to sleep.

CHAPTER FIVE

Friday morning slapped Edward wide awake, with Sparky's wet nose in the corner of his eye, a mere thirty-second before the alarm was set to go off. Edward was able to disable the clock before the incessant beeping began. Being awoken was at least a sign that he had slept somewhat, and for that, he was temporarily, mildly pleased.

However, he was far from having anything close to enough rest, and the non-sleep portion of the night was filled with rolling, twisting, and fighting with his covers— not to mention arm-wrestling his psyche. Some people have inner demons to contend with, but Edward had inner court jesters. Edward hadn't had a girlfriend since college. Any girl he ever liked, either paid him no mind at all or was outright mean to him. He learned early on just to set his sights a little lower.

Unexpectedly, he once dated an exchange student from Japan for an entire semester. Due to an ongoing miscommunication issue, she found him fascinating and amusing until her English improved and she broadened her circle of friends. That was when Naoko moved on to better things. At least, that was how Edward justified it to himself. Mostly, he assumed that any woman who would end up with him was choosing him as a third or fourth-round alternative to someone that had passed her by.

Even at the Hallowe'en party, Edward had had a drink to boost his self-assuredness and decided not to go for the loneliest looking woman in the room for a change. That didn't turn out well. Not to say that he could remember what happened exactly, but he didn't end up with her. Other events, including getting violently assaulted, took up the remainder of the evening.

The coffee maker had finished squeaking out the last tablespoon of exceptionally strong coffee into the pot. Edward poured himself a small cup, topped it with cream, and as usual, didn't stir it. He turned on the radio and opened the blinds. It was a surprisingly clear morning, which he interpreted as being cold.

The colder autumn days had fewer clouds, he had noticed. Perhaps a light sweater was in order.

The thought of Clotilde and the unavoidable conversations he would have with Daniel began to overtake him. The good news was that Edward wasn't as panic-stricken as he was when he first heard she had asked about him.

Could a nice woman like that actually be interested in me? Edward thought to himself. He relaxed significantly more when he firmly decided that there *must be* something wrong with her. There had to be.

Edward proceeded with his standard morning routine and made the required adjustments for his new eye-cleansing regimen. Edward looked slightly improved today; at least the inside of his eye didn't look as infected as it did the previous evening. The randomly distributed bruising around his eye was now a lurid yet sickly yellow outlined with just a hint of blue and purple. All he wanted was to make it through the day and unwind over the weekend. *Then everything would go back to normal.*

Sparky languished at the center of the kitchen table, cleansing himself luxuriously when Edward was almost ready to leave. "Geez, Sparky!" Disgusted, Edward shoed him off the table. Almost forgetting his leftovers, Edward made an about-face to the refrigerator, collected his containers, threw them and a pair of delicate black chopsticks into his snazzy, denim-looking reusable lunch bag that he borrowed from his camping gear. He was ready to be done with this week and pleasantly preoccupied to not have to think about Clotilde.

The difference between this Friday and the previous ones was not obvious to Edward at this time. It slipped along in the usual way except, of course, for the eyedrops, the black eye from having had the shit kicked out of him, subsequently having a woman enquire after him, and so forth. None of this was making its way to Edward's cognizance, not to mention all the deeper aspects of Edward's being, internal and external, that were affected, changed for better or worse.

He was no longer a man without a good scrap under his belt and a hell of a story that came along with it, which he still wasn't willing to tell. All the same, it was there. It was like a king who figuratively led his men but never went to battle, somehow less convincing. In Edward's case, he was alone, and it was not a pretty fight, nor was it heroic. If anyone had counted hits, Edward surely must have failed on every blow, surviving by his mere stature alone. He took a majestic beating and recovered, or was in the process of healing, surprisingly rather quickly.

He acquired the aid and attention of what appeared to be a fair and virtuous woman through the process. But still, Edward was unaware that things had changed, that by going to a party uncharacteristically alone, dressed as he was, he had set in motion a chain of events that either derailed his destiny or actualized it.

With all of Edward's denial and preoccupation with adhering to the routine, neither obsessively nor compulsively, he was happily moving ahead with his day. Animal Planet was on the TV for Sparky, the water turned off, one light on, crumbs scooped up, Edward even had time to take out his kitchen garbage on the way downstairs.

"Bye, Sparky. You be a good boy." He called from the front door. Sparky was already curled up on the sofa, holding the fort and pretending to ignore Edward. The deadbolt and doorknob locks were secured, and Edward unknowingly whistled to the elevator.

He pressed the "down" button, and not a second later, the doors opened. Mr.Whitley stampeded out and breathlessly blurted, "Oh gosh, I forgot my proposal! Had to come back up!" as he scurried past Edward, who hopped on, unfazed. Edward almost said something, but he often wasn't quick enough for spontaneous small-talk.

Edward pressed the basement button and continued whistling, only now, it was just in his head. Nobody came on, and Edward exited by the garage to throw out his garbage. There was an added chipper-ness to his step. He was usually in a good mood, but he was a little more delighted on this particular Friday.

When the icy air hit his face, Edward proudly reaffirmed that he *knew* it would be cold. Good thing he put on that sweater! Gloves on, collar up, shoulders edging towards earlobes, Edward scooted along the sidewalk, noticing that the puddles in the shade had iced over, but the ones touched by the sunlight were melted and drying up. The sun was low but strong, hitting one side of his face and occasionally reflecting off certain cars and straight into his eyes. Between the sun, the cold, and the pre-existing eye issues, a tear was being forced out the corner of his eye and slid back across his temple. He wiped it a couple of times, but it kept returning.

He could feel his phone vibrating in his pocket but did not want to remove his gloves until he reached work. He was almost there anyway. The phone repeatedly vibrated at short intervals; it was definitely Daniel.

People walked around on the sidewalk as if perfectly choreo-graphed; some were going the wrong way, not keeping to the right, determined or meandering at various speeds. Lights changed colours, and puddles were avoided; everyone's breath was visible, and there was the cold hum of typical morning commuter commotion.

The brushed metal lettering of Umonoteq looked golden in the sunlight, neutralizing its futuristic design. Edward never had feelings of fear or antagonism towards technology. Still, despite his age and innate skill, he was also not the type of person who believed that everything should be automated or that everyone should have robots in their smart homes that would be accessible at all times from mobile devices. He knew, better than most, that although the technology was hurtling into the future at unfathomable speed, it was also unreliable— not to mention unfixable by the average user.

Edward felt that he knew his place in the grand scheme of things, which was markedly several positions lower than where he should be, but he was forever underestimating himself. He was easy to satisfy on the surface but unaware that he longed for deeper connections. Daniel was the deepest connection he had to another human being. There he was, standing in the lobby, reaffixing his ponytail.

As if sensing Edward's presence, Daniel whirled around to face his friend, earbuds in and eyes darting, as one does when listening to someone talking, signally with a "shhh" gesture. Edward wasn't the type to interrupt what was obviously a phone call.

Between the 'uh-huh's,' it was clear that Daniel was examining Edward's eye and then gave him the thumbs up because it did look better. "Ok, ok, I gotta go. I can see him walking in." Daniel said to the person on the phone. Edward turned around to see who Daniel might have been referring to, but there was nobody that he recognized. Daniel made a series of indecipherable hand gestures. "OK bye, yeah, bye," and then clicked off and pulled the tiny white plugs from his ears, shoving the mess of wires into his pocket.

Heartily moving Edward towards the elevators, Daniel's eyebrows kept getting raised with something very conniving behind them. The elevator doors opened just as they arrived, and Edward knew Daniel was up to something. In all fairness, Daniel wasn't hiding it. In fact, he looked rather pleased with himself, but due to a jam-packed lift, he was waiting for some privacy to divulge freely.

"Are you going to tell me what you've got going on there?" Edward inquired dryly.

"Your eye looks great, by the way." Daniel turned to face the doors while everyone else quietly positioned themselves tightly in the elevator, all the while pretending not to listen.

"So, 'no.' Ok." Edward looked away and continued under his breath, "It's just that you look awfully pleased with yourself." They moved aside to let some people off, and Daniel loosened his posture now that more space was available. Edward turned his head to stare at him, but Daniel kept looking straight ahead. "You'll be happy. That's all I'm saying," gloated Daniel.

That was too much for Edward. There were still ten floors to go, and that was nine floors too many to wait to get the scoop. He started to feel a tad worried. "Oh no. What did you do?" Edward was back to speaking with his lips closed and stiff as if nobody else but Daniel could understand him. Daniel shrugged and tried to prevent his face from changing expression.

"Daniel. Who were you talking to?" Edward urged, but Daniel shrugged again. The remaining people pretended not to eavesdrop. "Really? You don't know who you were talking to?" The conversation could have been mistaken for a lovers' spat. Daniel said nothing but let out a slight whimper while having a more challenging time looking neutral. "I can see your eyes smiling. Was that *me*? The *'him'* you were referring to? 'I can see *him* walking in?'"

Daniel turned towards Edward with a twinkle in his eye. The last person, who exited to the floor before theirs, had to squeeze past them because Daniel and Edward had become oblivious to everyone else by this point. The instant the doors closed, Edward got louder, "Daniel, you're up to something, and I think I should be worried, and I don't know why. I mean, I know why; I know you, that's why." Daniel started to chuckle. "It was Clotilde!"

The elevator doors opened just as Edward blurted out, "What the fu—!" while Daniel confidently and briskly promenaded out with Edward floundering behind him. Judith was in her usual spot but was unable to catch their attention.

"Daniel!" Edward whispered loudly as he swiftly trailed behind Daniel down their row of cubicles. Daniel happily ignored Edward until he reached his chair, delicately took off his scarf and coat, and placed them softly on the hook.

At his wit's end, Edward stooped slightly, grabbed his buddy by the shoulders and whispered angrily, "Daniel, I've never seen you take so much care in hanging up your stuff. Could you please tell me who the fuck you were talking to... just tell me already before I go insane!" Edward tried to bend at the knees so nobody would see him on the verge of throttling his best friend.

Excruciatingly pleased with himself, Daniel smirked, "*Before* you go insane?"

"Daniel!" Edward's whisper was a bit too loud; some heads turned, and he ducked and continued probing. "Daniel, I swear to god, will you just spill the beans already!"

"Spill the beans?"

"Yes. All the beans."

"Ok." Daniel conceded; Edward loosened his grip and almost melted away with relief.

Daniel quietly, proudly, continued, "I texted my sister when I got up this morning, knowing she was probably finishing her night shift at seven— with Clotilde somewhere around there. My sister called me right back from the work phone."

Edward didn't blink, "And how did you get to talking with Clotilde?"

"I'm getting there. Geez! I told my sister you liked Clotilde and were thinking of asking her out, and then something happened and she quickly handed the phone to Clotilde saying, 'it's my brother' and then she got on the phone."

"You told your sister *I liked her*?! That's crazy. I don't even *know* her!" Edward was thoroughly embarrassed.

"Dude! You said you didn't want my sister to be the go-between. So I figured *somebody* had to be because if we left it up to you, you'd have to get injured just to meet her again!"

"No, I wouldn't! I'd probably just forget about it." Edward admitted sheepishly.

"Proving my point!" Daniel felt justified and continued, "so anyway, I asked if she remembered you, and she said yes, and I asked if it would be ok if you gave her a call. Then she asked if you had asked me to call her, and I said no, you didn't have any idea."

"Which is true."

"Yeah, so she said it would be better to keep up with the story, that *she* asked *my sister* for your number. So it wouldn't look suspicious, on my part."

"Ok nice. But you're telling me."

"Yeah, I'm your friend, which you fail to realize sometimes. So I gave her your number, and she's gonna call you. And for the record, she's not supposed to do that - they can't fraternize with their patients; it's against the rules." Daniel, able to fully relax and move freely, patted Edward on the arm before turning to sit down.

Edward stood blankly for an eternity behind Daniel, who was in the process of starting up his computer. Everything was moving so fast. One moment he was dealing with an infected eye from a Hallowe'en party brawl, and the next minute he was getting set up with an auburn-haired rule-breaker. It was dizzying.

"Edward, it's gonna be fine. Just get to work. Thank me later."

Edward wanted to argue desperately. He couldn't, though, because the truth was that Daniel was right. If Daniel hadn't done what he did, Edward would probably never make a move. It was too awkward to encounter someone at their workplace and such an important and serious workplace environment at that. Not that it wasn't any less awkward at this moment, but there was at least some progress with the bonus of having to keep it a secret.

Befuddled, Edward wandered over to his desk. Entirely on autopilot, he began to boot up everything like any typical morning and placed his coat and backpack where they belonged. He sat staring at his screen, not budging, his mind elsewhere, when out of nowhere, a sharp, penetrating voice spoke beside him.

"Hey, Ed." It was Judith. Edward flinched in his seat like a kid watching a horror movie and let out an equally childish squeal in fright. He slowly swivelled around to glare at Judith, who was undeniably amused. "Sorry; I didn't mean to scare you, Eddie."

With the slow, perturbed blink, "Edward." He corrected her for the billionth time. "You didn't 'scare' me, I was just trying to solve a problem, and I didn't hear you."

"Whatever. Listen, I am going to propose something to the new division head when he starts, and I wanted to run it by you." Judith went straight to the point.

Daniel wheeled himself over closer to Edward's cubicle. Judith continued while Edward tried to look like he couldn't care less. "I want to create a core team within this floor to handle more specialty products; things that involve more security, creativity, innovation, and was wondering if you'd be interested."

Edward was profoundly flattered but couldn't bring himself to show it. He began to look at Judith with suspicion, pursing his lips as he tapped a finger on his desk. Was this just a ploy to make her look good to the new people so she could move up, or was Judith genuinely interested in creating a team of equals?

"Ed, yes or no? You're good at this stuff and fast." She burrowed her laser beam eyes into his skull.

Daniel piped up, "I'll do it," he offered. Judith slowly turned to Daniel, said nothing, and turned back to Edward, "Well?"

Edward, still doubtful that this was a genuine offer, asked, "Can I think about it?" as he attempted to glare back at her, finger still tapping as he funnelled all of his nervous energy into that finger.

"There's nothing to think about; it's a hypothetical situation unless somebody goes for it."

"Ok, well, would it pay more?" Edward wanted to feel like he was negotiating instead of jumping whenever Judith said 'boo'.

"Obviously."

"Yeah, ok."

"Cool." Judith unfolded her arms. She knew Edward would agree from the start and wondered why he bothered wasting her time. "Don't tell anyone," she warned sternly.

Without waiting for confirmation, Judith spun around, marched away, and disappeared behind the cubicles.

Daniel's ego was slightly wounded, but he shrugged it off and went back to work. As for Edward, the abruptness of Judith's visit was exactly what he needed to be thrust back into the tasks at hand.

It never took too long for Edward to become enthralled by his work. It wasn't because it was incredibly fascinating, but whenever he started, it would quickly engulf him. By the time lunch break rolled around, which was often precisely the amount of time it took to become bug-eyed or hungry or both and so a natural pause and stretch would occur.

Sometimes things got glitchy, and either he or Daniel could be heard grumbling to themselves. They would take coffee breaks together for the most part. Daniel often led the way in that regard. It wasn't that he was lazier than Edward, but he paid more attention to his self-care.

Today, Edward grumbled and moved forward systematically until lunchtime. By the change in sounds coming from his cubicle, the clicks switched to shuffling; Daniel knew that it was lunchtime and called over, "I brought food today. You?"

Edward yawned, "Yeah. Leftovers."

"Me too. My mom loaded me up with stuff."

Edward stood up with a full stretch and stifled a yawn. He wiped his eyes, twisted and cracked some joints in his back and neck.

Daniel popped around the wall, "Ever do yoga?" It was the sort of comment that didn't require a reply; he was merely observing how Edward was winding himself up like a pretzel one way and then in the opposite direction.

"I don't know why I'm so tired. All these carbs I brought are going to knock me out this afternoon!" He grabbed his lunch bag. Edward genuinely forgot that he slept poorly the night before. Then he looked at his phone and remembered that Clotilde had his number.

Daniel spied the subtleness of Edward's glance as Edward slipped the phone into his pocket.

"If she's anything like my sister, she's probably gone home and went straight to sleep," Daniel assured him.

Pretending he had no idea what Daniel was talking about, Edward let out an exaggerated, "Huh?" and then fussed with his belongings unnecessarily.

Playing along just a little, Daniel explained, "Clotilde. I doubt she'll call right away after such a long shift."

"Oh, yeah. I doubt she'll call today." Edward agreed as if he wasn't looking forward to her call whatsoever. Indeed, what he felt was that he _doubted_ if she would call today _or ever_. The pair walked down their aisle towards the elevators. There was a set of swinging doors just past them that led to a hallway, private offices, washrooms, and a lunchroom.

Prolonged silence made Daniel uncomfortable, and he started to babble about his mother and all the food she had tried to give him, the multitude of questions she had, and the litany of complaints she made. Edward didn't make his usual effort to pay attention and appeared distant. That just made Daniel talk faster as he hopped from point to point.

They had the lunchroom mostly to themselves. Once they had both heated their food in the microwave, Daniel sat down and sprawled his meal out before him. Conversely, Edward stood, leaning up against the wall holding his container close to his chest while shovelling food into his mouth with his chopsticks. He could see that his 'not sitting' was causing an increasing amount of discomfort in Daniel.

It was bad enough that Edward was 'freakishly tall' as Daniel would put it, but now his towering beside and slightly behind Daniel did not allow for sufficient relaxation for which to eat and not cause indigestion. Daniel eventually insisted that Edward sit, and to usher forth 'the end of it', Edward complied and Daniel was visibly comforted.

As nerdy, compliant, and polite as Edward was generally, his table manners had fallen away after eating so many meals at night alone. He tended to shovel food in, chomp boisterously, and with carnivorous speed. Daniel looked on in amazement.

Edward was oblivious to Daniel's stupefaction and continued eating with no less enthusiasm until every morsel was consumed. He then hopped up, briskly rinsed his containers in the sink, wiped his mouth and hands off with water, and sat back down to wait for Daniel to finish.

Daniel was only about halfway through his meal when he observed, "you'd probably have no problem surviving in the bush."

"What do you mean?" Edward was confused. It seemed an odd comment for Daniel to make at this particular moment. He observed Daniel slowly dine on his leftovers.

"Like, you could go totally Grizzly Adams." Daniel didn't look up but steadily kept consuming.

Edward thought about it for a second more, "Uh, no, I don't think so. You mean like go live in the wilderness?" He had no idea where it was coming from. Daniel hardly paid attention now that he could eat unbothered by Edward's dominant eating style. Daniel's eating style was very passive, were it not for the fact he was feeding himself. The food appeared to be slowly coaxed into Daniel's mouth versus Edward's more ravenous, predatory way of devouring his meal.

After a few more seconds of silence, while Edward actually tried to imagine what Daniel was talking about, Daniel scraped one of his containers clean, Edward continued, "Well, I *was* in Boy

Scouts when I was a kid." Daniel nodded knowingly and still refrained from looking up.

"But as far as living off-grid in a cabin, I don't know. I don't think I could do that. What made you think of it?" Edward asked.

"Oh, just that you seem to have instincts that you don't even know you have." Daniel was referring to the eating, of course, and possibly the fight. Edward shrugged. He was open to the possibility of having instincts that may or may not kick in at the appropriate time, but in reality, as far as they had appeared so far, they hadn't truly made themselves known to Edward at all.

To be that naturally in-tune as a male of the species, a hunter or gatherer, problem-solver or protector, these were undoubtedly unknown character traits completely hidden from Edward's consciousness. He would love for nothing more than such latent instincts to kick in at some point of crisis, but they hadn't so far. If it weren't for his ability to manipulate technology, Edward felt that he had no skills whatsoever. He was good with cats, but it was nothing that any old, crazy cat-lady wouldn't have easily acquired.

The pair finished up in the lunchroom, and they both obediently tidied up their end of the table. Upon reaching the maximum minutes of silence that he was comfortable with, Daniel asked, "What do you think is up with Judith and that 'team thing' she was talking about before?"

"I don't know. I never know if she's just messing with me." Edward admitted as they walked past Judith's desk back to their cubicles. Daniel understood Edward's suspicions of Judith, although he didn't quite feel the same way about her, at least not to the same intensity as Edward. They didn't know enough about Judith to know if she was ethical or not.

She was like a venomous snake that was shrewd and probably had nothing against you personally. Still, like mythological serpents, she possessed superior knowledge and abilities that humans couldn't comprehend, nor could they ever possess. The only friends of such creatures would have to be other venomous snakes because humans who clumsily walked upright and who had opposable thumbs were such easy prey for the potentially deadly, silent, slithering, strategist without arms, legs, fin, or feather.

So, of course, Edward didn't trust her. He couldn't. She asked for his help to be part of a team. That in itself was odd because, as far as Edward believed, Judith didn't need a team. Daniel suggested, "You know, maybe she just wants to *look* like a team-player for the new department head."

"Yeah, who knows. She makes me nervous. I don't think she needs input from any of us." Edward grumbled.

Daniel agreed but continued, "Well, she doesn't have enough hours in the day to do everybody's job, so I'm sure she needs us for something. Or needs *you* for something; she didn't care to include me in the hypothetical team."

"True. But she just makes me feel like I'm so dumb. Like I'm a pet like Sparky or something."

"But, Sparky's a cat, and as we both know, he actually runs the show!" Daniel pointed out, hoping to boost Edward's self-esteem.

"Ok then, not Sparky. That's a bad example. Sparky most definitely feels far superior to me." He paused and continued, "I feel like a goldfish - swimming around in circles feeling like I'm doing something significant in my plastic castle. But in the end, I'm just blowing bubbles."

Edward stood at his cubicle, staring at Daniel, who concluded that although he bore little resemblance to an actual goldfish, Edward was accurate in his feelings. They both sighed, and settled into their respective work stations aspiring to remain sufficiently alert for the final few hours of an intense week.

CHAPTER SIX

Edward managed to stay awake despite the dozy lure of a massive carbohydrate-laden lunch. It was an ill-advised choice for a Friday. Regardless, it was 4:57 pm; he made it through and not only had he been as productive as usual, he hadn't thought about Clotilde even once— until just then.

Was it the mere novelty of the situation that captivated Edward so intensely, or was it the specific interest in Clotilde herself? He didn't know, not consciously, anyway. Subconsciously, however, although Edward hadn't been actively looking for a woman, he had only hoped, in the opaquest corners of his psyche, that one would eventually fall out the sky and be presented to him. This was as close to that scenario as one could get.

On an instinctual level, Edward was unequivocally interested in Clotilde for dozens of reasons beyond her inexplicable interest in him. She was, of course, physically attractive in a pleasant, natural, and symmetrical sort of way. One could suggest that she was even the female equivalent to Edward: taller than average, understated, intelligent, educated, stable, and easy-going. But for the time being, Edward still felt that she was somewhat out of his league, for Clotilde was also assertive, and Edward thought he was not.

For the most part, Edward was adequately assertive when it came to things of a practical nature like going to school, applying for jobs, renting an apartment, or ordering food. In terms of his relationships or his nonexistent love life, he floated around like a rudderless dinghy on a duck pond.

Truth be told, Edward was yearning to know everything about Clotilde, but such feelings were not permitted to waft into conscious thought just yet. There was still the belief that if Clotilde had a prolonged sincere interest in Edward, it was due to some form of dysfunction in her. This inference stemmed from Edward's lifelong ability to attract strays of all types. He had a flair for accumulating a variety of misfits and welcoming them to his inner circle.

It was a wonderful quality Edward possessed, and although he didn't judge those he collected, he was fully aware of their failings and impediments. Thus, he expected that Clotilde would prove to be no different if she were to maintain an interest in him. What those impediments were, and whether they were tolerable or not, remained to be seen. Edward concluded that the likelihood was actually the worst-case scenario in which Clotilde lacked any such impediment and, consequently, would lose interest in him as quickly as she had acquired it.

It was just a matter of going through the motions until such an outcome came to fruition. Edward was deep in thought when he finally clued into Daniel's excessive throat clearing.

"Are you trying to get my attention?" Edward asked as he slowly turned around in his chair.

"It's Friday, and the day is over, dude. What are you daydreaming about?" Daniel jested with an immature, idiotic grin on his face.

Edward didn't bite. "I'm just sleepy after all those carbs; it was hard to stay awake," which wasn't entirely untrue.

Daniel played along, "Did you manage to finish filling out the data-sheet for Charles?"

"Yep. Just a few minutes ago." Edward began his shutdown protocol. Unknowingly, he let out a woeful sigh as he sluggishly put everything away. It wasn't just the carbs that had exhausted him; it was the entire week's escapades that had done him in. But lastly, while his cognitive faculties occupied themselves with actual work, it was his innermost self that had been conducting an extensive investigation into his love life, that ultimately was responsible for the last knockout round. Edward was completely unaware of this.

Daniel, on the other hand, surmised that Edward might be feeling somewhat anxious about Clotilde's impending phone call.

Knowing how his anxiety had a tendency to wear himself down, he asked, "So I guess she hasn't called yet?"

Edward tried unsuccessfully to appear nonchalant, "Uh, who, Clotilde?" Daniel raised his eyebrows as if to say, 'who else?'. Edward continued fumbling with his computer, looked down and shrugged, "No, obviously, you would have heard my phone. I mean, as you said, she probably does the same thing as your sister."

Everything was put away, and by the time Edward had put his coat on and collected his things, Daniel was just standing against the window waiting for him, staring pitifully. When Edward finally looked at Daniel's concerned expression, he didn't want to admit that it could be warranted.

"What?" Edward thrust his chin forward.

Daniel volleyed back, upping the ante by gesturing with his hands. "What?" They stared at each other for a moment. "C'mon, let's get out of here." He grabbed Edward by the shoulder and led him towards the exit.

Some things were not necessary to articulate. Daniel knew that Edward had worked himself to death in his mind about everything that had transpired that week and Edward knew that Daniel understood that he *did* feel pitiful, if not slightly pathetic. None of these words would ever be exchanged aloud.

There was a jovial air about the office as people were making plans for the evening and weekend. As much as Daniel tried to get invited to things and be at the hub, Edward tried in the opposite direction. Edward wouldn't have had any idea of the office goings-on if it weren't for Daniel's gossiping. From Edward's perspective, he was surrounded by a group of averagely boring geeks, whereas Daniel saw himself amidst a thriving, long-running soap opera.

At the last moment, they encountered Judith. The last dreaded moment of Edward's day.

"Hey, Eddie!" Judith blurted out as Edward and Daniel stood facing the elevators. Edward recoiled and turned to face her. He bit his lip and glared because he could not bring himself to correct her one more time this week. Judith winked and continued, "Don't forget what we talked about. You're still on board, right?"

Edward made a visibly confused and irritated expression, "Yes," as he swung back to get into the elevator with Daniel.

Judith reminded them, "Because the new guy starts Monday."

Edward couldn't be bothered to hide his disdain and muttered under his breath, a garbled version of, "God, what's she on about, she can't ever get my name right, Jesus." Daniel waved goodbye to Judith but looked on with surprise at Edward. It was unusual for Edward to be so obviously aggravated.

"Dude, what's up? I mean, I know she never gets your name right, but you seem extra peeved." Daniel enquired.

"I am extra peeved," Edward admitted, trying just to let it go and be his usual, passive self.

It sufficiently appeased Daniel, "Fair enough." as he patted Edward on his back. They remained silent throughout their descent to the lobby, while people from every floor crammed into the closet-like elevator.

As if each level brought Edward's anxiety down a notch, he was almost completely relaxed by the time they exited. Edward turned and twisted his neck, making it crack loudly, signalling further progress towards total relaxation. Daniel, who habitually cracked his knuckles loudly and with disregard, could not stand other people cracking anything.

"Ugh, dude, you shouldn't do that." He cringed.

"*You* do it." Edward countered.

"Yeah, not my neck, though. You'll do that one day, and snap your spinal cord and then fall to the ground like a piece of limp spaghetti," he warned as he waved his hands around imitating what a limp spaghetti would look like. Edward stopped walking and just stared at him. Daniel just stared back.

"And you wonder why you didn't get into medicine," said Edward sarcastically as he started walking again towards the main doors.

Daniel, a second behind, rushed up beside him, "I didn't get *in*, because I didn't *wish* to get into medicine. But you could always ask my sister about paralyzing yourself; she'll tell ya", they exited the building and started along the sidewalk. Daniel continued mocking Edward playfully, who pretended to be angry. The banter was good for him.

"Or," Daniel continued, wide-eyed, "you know who you could ask? You could ask Clotilde!" He began almost skipping to keep up with Edward, who could walk fast comfortably due to his naturally long strides. Edward maintained his focus, "Shut up."

Delighted, Daniel persisted, "Yeah, you could ask Clotilde and see if she'd still wanna date you if you were paralyzed from the chin down." Edward almost lost his poker face.

"Well, I don't even know if she's interested in dating me *un*-paralyzed, so let's drop it." Edward accidentally admitted.

Realizing that Edward had not intended to divulge his feelings on the subject in that way at that time, Daniel stopped joking. "It's ok. It'll be fine."

"Shut up." Edward insisted in the politest way.

"What's not to like? She's gonna totally dig you."

"Oh, for God's sake." Edward just didn't know how to get Daniel off the topic. "Can we just stop talking about her?!"

But Daniel insisted, "No, but seriously—"

"Seriously *what*?! Stop talking about it, *please*!" Edward stopped walking and was almost shouting at Daniel. Daniel was unbothered. He was happy and content when people were yelling. Their mutual stare was suddenly interrupted by the ringing emanating from Edward's breast pocket. They resumed staring at each other with much wider eyes, realizing as Murphy's Law would have it, that was most likely Clotilde.

"Answer it! Answer it!" Whispered Daniel while waving maniacally.

Edward couldn't easily get to his pocket with his gloves on, as the rings were taunting him like a buzzer in a game show. He was running out of time. He pulled the glove off with his teeth, reached into his pocket with lightning speed, but unfortunately not with lightning accuracy, and the phone slipped out of his grasp onto the sidewalk in front of him. Wholly immersed in urgency and chaos, Edward's right foot kicked the phone another meter ahead in one swift knee-jerk reaction. As the two friends scrambled towards it, uttering a litany of expletives, Daniel cheered words of encouragement, "It's still ringing; it's still ringing!" Then Edward finally clasped the phone solidly in his hand and pressed the "accept" button.

Breathlessly, and perhaps desperately, he declared, "Hello?!" and paused as Daniel stood expectantly. "Hello?" Edward repeated as breathlessly as the first time.

"*Edward?*" The voice on the phone said, sounding confused.

Trying to regain his composure Edward looked over to Daniel to alert him with subtle eye cues that it was a woman, probably Clotilde. "Uh, yes, this is Edward."

Daniel made exaggerated motions directing Edward to breathe deeply, which of course, had the opposite effect on Edward, as it was very distracting to watch.

The female voice said, "Is this a bad time? You sound out of breath."

"No, no it's fine. I just... I was just... it was actually, well, a funny thing happened..." Edward giggled nervously and had a difficult time collecting his thoughts while Daniel was waving furiously for him to get off this train of thought. Again, it wasn't overly helpful.

"Uh, never mind... so who is calling?" said Edward, becoming overly formal. Daniel cringed.

"It's Clotilde!" She said with an unmistakable smile in her voice.

Edward tried painfully not to sound excited, but that only made him sound odd. "Ohhh, Clotilde. Yes, hello." He raised his eyebrows repeatedly at Daniel, who was seriously deciding whether or not to have a heart attack and be done with the agony of watching this unfold.

Edward turned away so as not to be distracted by Daniel. He tried to relax and sound normal, but Clotilde had to ask again, "Are you sure everything's ok?"

"Yes! I was just leaving work with my... co-worker, and I was just heading home." Edward spoke unusually slow and clear as if he was on a tech support call with an elderly person. Then to clarify, quickly, Edward blurted, "I mean I'm not headed home with him, I'm headed home alone. So I'm free." At this point, Edward was about to have a heart attack of his own, and Daniel walked around to be in front of him again.

"Ok... well, technically, it's not only inappropriate but also not allowed for me to call you because you were my patient in the hospital..."

Edward suddenly reverted to a five-year-old version of himself. He stood there holding the phone as if it was a balloon that just got popped with a giant pin. He stood, frozen. Edward understood Clotilde's statement to mean that she was sorry to inform him that she was unable to pursue anything except a professional relationship with him, or at least that was the excuse she was using not to see him.

"Hello?" Clotilde continued because Edward hadn't said anything but looked vacantly at Daniel.

"Yes! Yes, hello." Edward mumbled, feigning enthusiasm while Daniel wilted with uncertainty beside him.

"So, you have to promise me you will never come back to the emerge." Clotilde continued playfully but in all seriousness.

Not fully grasping was Clotilde had said, Edward obediently obliged, "I will never come back to the emerge."

"Great! Now that we got that out of the way, would you like to go out for a drink or something?" Clotilde still sounded like she was smiling. Edward was a bit slow in this department, and so it took him a moment longer than it should have to respond, but he managed to utter, with a palpable sigh of relief, "Ohh, haha! I see what you're saying. Haha."

Daniel was resuscitated by this but was embarrassed for Edward, who, in his opinion, sounded ridiculous. "What? What?" he mouthed at Edward and signalled with hand gestures to wrap it up so as not to ruin it altogether.

"How about this evening then? Or is that too soon?" Edward was taking one step back for every step forward. It was painful for Daniel to watch.

"No, it's not too soon for me. Is it too soon for you?" Clotilde was almost outright giggling.

"No, it's fine. I have nothing better to do." Edward stated confidently, but Daniel slapped himself in the forehead in disbelief.

"I mean, I'm available. Completely available this evening." Edward also began to feel what Daniel had been feeling.

"Good. Is there any place that you prefer to go?" Clotilde asked.

"Uh, no. No, I think my judgment in that area is a little off, as you may know." Edward laughed and snorted. "You decide."

"Well, there's a place on 4th that's nice. I can text you the address, and we could meet at seven?" Suggested Clotilde calmly.

"Seven is good. Great. Thank you." Edward was happy to wrap it up as quickly as possible before Clotilde realized she had made a terrible mistake.

"OK. See you soon." She said.

"OK, bye, thank-you. Bye." Edward just could not get the hang of this conversation.

The call ended and he looked very pleased with himself. Daniel, who almost passed out through the ordeal, banged his forehead into Edward's shoulder repeatedly, muttering, "Jesus Christ, Edward. That was unbelievable. If you said 'thank you' one more time, I was gonna rip your larynx out."

CHAPTER SEVEN

Edward appeared calm on the surface. Any onlookers would not know of the molten lava that was pumping through his veins. But Daniel knew. In fact, Daniel contributed to it greatly.

"Thank-you? Really?" Daniel grilled him.

Edward started to pace on the sidewalk. "Did I really sound that pathetic?" He looked at Daniel with an expression that was halfway between humiliation and optimism. "Oh god, I did. I did. Why does she still want to go out with me? I am so not good at this. I'm better in person." Edward looked to Daniel again to gain some assurance. "Aren't I?"

Finally, Daniel piped in, "Yes! Yes, in-person you'll be fine. Anyway, when she sees you again, she'll see how you're just a big lanky nerd and not some asshole with a black eye."

Then it dawned on Edward that perhaps the only reason Clotilde was even interested in him at all was due to the black eye. Maybe she thought he was some kind of bad boy.

"Oh no. Do you think *that's* why she wants to go out with me? Maybe she thought I was this 'bad-boy' who gets into fights and stuff?"

"Edward, I highly doubt that." Daniel tried to ground him. "Listen, just go home. This way." He turned Edward in the opposite direction. "Go home, have a shower. Put on clean clothes. Maybe even have a little drink."

Edward nodded in agreement until the last part. "I don't have anything left to drink, and I just don't feel like that's such a good idea just yet."

"Dude! What the hell happened to you at that party?" Daniel realized he still hadn't been caught up to speed on the traumatizing event.

"It's not important now. I'm going to just go home and get this over with." Edward started walking again. Daniel chased after him.

"Wait, wait! Edward, enjoy yourself, for God's sake. It's nothing to 'get over with'. It's not a frikkin' root canal!" Daniel began to lose his composure again.

"Yeah, I know. I mean this part. All the thinking about it part: I'm just gonna go and meet her. It'll be fine. I'm sure you're right." Edward took exaggerated deep breaths between thoughts. It wasn't apparent if he was trying to convince Daniel or himself. They nodded to each other as if heading off to battle. Daniel turned to go in the opposite direction.

"OK, text me after," Daniel shouted.

Edward just waved back at him and continued walking. He walked as quickly as he could without running. He focused on every minuscule detail that captured his eye so as not to worry about thousands of plausible eventualities.

There was a large part of him that still hadn't reconciled what had happened at the party. He wasn't a big drinker, but a regular one, who never got drunk. But, for some reason that night between his drinking and poorly chosen, unintentionally offensive costume, Edward got the beating of his life. He wasn't too eager to relive any part of it or for right now, ruining another perfectly good evening.

As for his date with Clotilde, Edward just wanted to survive it. Just let her not hate him by the end of it. Not a religious person, Edward was petitioning as many deities, from as many religions, as he could think of.

Upon reaching his apartment, Edward began recounting the whole tale to Sparky, who seemed oddly interested. It was the best time to communicate with Sparky because he was starved for affection all day. Edward rushed around, closed the blinds, threw his coat on the sofa, and put his lunch containers on the kitchen counter. He scattered everything he came in with over a wide area in an attempt to get ready as quickly as possible.

"Gotta shower, Sparky. I don't have time to chit chat." But Sparky just sat in the hallway unbothered, grooming himself.

Through the venting hole in the bathroom ceiling, Edward could hear the mysterious voices of the people who lived upstairs, which was soon drowned out by the running water in his shower. He started off with it rather hot and then made it colder the longer he stayed in there. He couldn't even remember if he had washed his hair yet or not, so he rewashed it just to be sure. Edward also decided to do his eye treatment right away in order to look his best possible, all things considered.

He couldn't stop mumbling to himself and narrated his every move to Sparky as if he was out in the hallway with a stopwatch. Edward was unaware that Sparky was already nestled on Edward's pillow.

"Drying myself now, Sparky. Gonna do my eye stuff next. We got this." Edward was highly skittish. "Deodorant! Let's do deodorant first." The realization that he might be suffering from excessive perspiration was a good call. Edward applied his 'patchouli-scented natural deodorant for men' with masterful attention.

"Ok, now the eye." Edward stared at himself in the mirror with his extra-large plush green towel wrapped around his gangly, almost translucent midsection. His well-formed ribs reflected the bathroom light like a modest suit of armour. Edward scanned his cadaverous complexion north to south and back again, and squinted as he tousled his damp hair with his fingertips. With the slightest air of confidence, whispered to the Edward in the mirror, "I don't know; I think you totally rocked Goth Jesus."

With that, Edward proceeded with his eye treatment, dried off, and went into the bedroom to select suitable first date attire. Sparky peeked through his sleepy eyes for only a second to acknowledge Edward's presence, then resumed his posture, emulating a tightly rolled cinnamon bun.

There were clean shirts on the laundry basket, but they weren't ironed. Unless he chose a t-shirt or another type of shirt that didn't need ironing, going wrinkled wasn't the kind of casual Edward was aiming for. He suddenly realized that he hadn't checked his phone for Clotilde's text message to have an inkling of how to dress for the venue they were going to.

Edward scuttled back down the hall to get his coat. He rifled through his pocket and was hugely relieved as soon as he saw there was one new message.

"Hi. Here's the place: The Sovereign Pub on 4th. See you @7" with a winking face emoticon.

Edward was about to map it immediately but realized he should probably reply first. He was happy that he hadn't seen it until now, so he could appear to look less eager, especially after the wink. How a simplistic winking yellow circle could make him this excited, was beyond his comprehension.

He replied: "Thanks, see you @7"

He wondered if he should wink back. Instead, he opted for a 'thumbs up' icon. He risked appearing just friendly, but that was much better than the alternative. If Edward didn't hold back now, there would be no chance later.

Edward began to map the location when Clotilde instantly texted him back with a 'thumbs up' as well. This made him feel much more secure. The map app calculated that he could walk to the location in 20 minutes. In Edward's opinion, these estimates were for short people who strolled; he always could knock anywhere from thirty to fifty percent off the time without even being close to breaking a sweat.

If he were to leave his place by 6:40, he would arrive early or on time. Edward felt very much in control for the first time in days. He swaggered back to his room, swung off his towel, and began to get dressed. Was it corduroy weather or dressy jeans? Plaid or striped shirt? Should he layer, or go skinny? This dressing thing was more complicated than he anticipated.

There were many factors to consider. What was clean and what looked good on him. What would be warm enough, but not too warm. What kind of place was it and how were the other people dressed? He put on his dark socks and underwear and ran back to his phone. Sparky buried his head in the duvet.

Edward decided to check out the website for the pub. It was comforting to find out it looked like an old English pub. Edward scampered back to his room; he knew exactly what to wear. His wardrobe was made for this place. In the last second before leaping into his room like a spring deer, his sock caught a tiny nail on the metal strip that sealed the seam of the hall carpet to the bedroom carpet.

It might as well have been a bear trap. Edward's snagged sock held his leg in place while the rest of him was catapulted forward only to result in a face plant onto the floor. Sparky ran for cover.

"Shit! Shit. Shit." Edward let out a delayed response; his foot, by way of his sock, was still attached to the nail in the floor, and his chin was starting to sting. Spinning around on the floor gracefully, from his stomach to his back, sitting up and then wiggling his way toward the pinned sock, Edward had the slightest inclination to stay home. He unhooked his sock, stood up, and with his heart racing, shook it off and told himself out loud, "OK, it's fine, it's nothing. You're ok; you're just not paying attention. You're still going. Just keep going."

Sparky resurfaced as Edward hopped up and down, shaking his arms loose and tilting his head from left to right. He was going to keep with it and follow through. He ignored the pulled yarn in his favorite dressy, winter socks, and put on his dressy jeans, a thin, slim-fitted, buttoned-down plaid shirt and a blue-grey pullover with a hood.

He put on an antique wristwatch that belonged to his grandfather. The black leather strap was weathered with masculinity and fitted snuggly with the brushed silver edge that held the large and very thin beveled face. It anchored Edward.

One last trip to the bathroom, Edward looked in the mirror, tousled his hair, which was mostly dry now. He decided not to put on any additional fragrance, and he then made sure that his watch and his phone were synchronized. It was almost time to leave. Teeth brushed, bladder emptied, fly up, hands washed— he was actually ready.

Edward was going on a date with a real live woman. His chin was still stinging and he now felt that he might have bruised his knee as well, but he persevered. He very slowly collected his keys, his wallet, his phone, got his coat on and headed towards the door.

"Bye, Sparky! Don't wait up!" Edward chuckled to himself. Like that would happen! A date was one thing, but he wasn't delusional. There was no way that this would be anything more than a friendly first date. It might even be an only date, for all Edward knew. He didn't want to jinx it.

While most people braced themselves for the cold, Edward welcomed it. It helped him relax. He was careful not to skip or hop or stub his toe on the way; so he walked fast, but more conscientiously than usual. The way this week had gone, he didn't want to show up with a broken nose or covered in puddle water.

The sky was elegantly adorned like strewn diamonds on black velvet, but again, Edward didn't let it distract him too much. He arrived at the pub and pulled out his phone to let Clotilde know he arrived. It was 6:56 pm.

Edward was about to text her when Clotilde materialized in front of him. Edward was taken aback; Clotilde was more bewitching than he remembered. She smiled warmly. Edward attempted to verbalize his thoughts, but no words made their way out.

Thankfully Clotilde was more expressive. "You're early too! When did you get here?" She asked delightedly.

"Just now. I was going to text you." Words began to flow better for Edward, although he couldn't stop staring at her with sheer wonderment.

"Shall we go in?" She suggested, motioning to the door.

"No, I think I like it out here," Edward replied. It's something sarcastic he would typically say to Daniel, but never would he be so bold to say that so soon into a first date. He immediately started to panic and regretted that he had made the joke.

But Clotilde started to laugh. "You're funny. Don't you want a drink?" Edward was loosening up with wild abandon, which completely blind-sided him. It was as if he was taken over by an alter ego. "Drink? Hmm. As long as you promise not to punch me in the eye."

"I promise." Said Clotilde. She seemed genuinely tickled by Edward, and they proceeded to go into the pub. Edward continued mumbling behind her, "Yeah, 'cause I'm not allowed to go to the ER now. But if you punch me, the deal's off, lady!" Where was this coming from? Edward was amazed at himself - he was usually terrible at banter. He decided to cool it for a while, just in case he started to say moronic things again.

Clotilde entered the vestibule and stopped. It was a small area. Edward was suddenly right up behind her and could smell her freshly washed hair. He couldn't get over how intoxicating she was. She had a sympathetic and pleasant smile whenever she spoke.

"Have you ever been here before?" She asked, "Where do you want to sit?"

"No, I have never been here before, and let's sit somewhere tall." Edward spied some higher tables with barstools. "If that's ok with you?" he added, somewhat shyly and politely, not wanting to dictate where they sat based solely on his own personal preference.

Clotilde agreed, and they walked over to the tall tables. The entire encounter thus far was surreal to Edward. Something terrible was about to happen, and based on the level of 'good' that had been going on, it would have to be proportionately bad. In any other realm, Edward would not be this cynical. It was only with his love life that he felt it just would never happen in a great way or even in a good way. It *could* happen, in a satisfactory manner, eventually.

They took off their coats and hung them on the backs of their chairs. Edward gazed at Clotilde until she took notice.

Still giggling, "What? You're staring at me." She said uncomfortably.

Edward felt embarrassed as he wasn't aware he had been staring. "Sorry!" He stated and quickly looked away.

"What is it?" She asked again.

"Nothing." Edward kept his eyes down on the drinks menu. "I was just noticing..." Edward searched the recesses of his mind as if it was listed on the menu, "What a nice and unbruised complexion you have."

"Oh! Haha! Well, you know, if that was taken out of context, that could sound totally creepy!" Clotilde noted and laughed.

Edward looked up over the menu, softening his eyes, "Uh...yeah, you're right... sorry. Especially since I did NOT meet you in the hospital."

"You most certainly DIDN'T meet me in the hospital."

"Agreed."

Edward must have reread the beer list eight or nine times, without actually grasping any of it, when the waiter walked over. He was a thin, chiselled, intense, artsy type, wearing a white t-shirt that looked like it was painted on. The sleeves were rolled up, exposing a variety of tattoos. His presence rattled Edward.

"Hi, Chloë! How's it going?" His smile was wide and boasted a row of perfect, bleached teeth, sandwiched between perfect dimples on each cheek. He flipped his hair and posed like a model in a figure drawing class. *'Chloë'?* He sounded awfully familiar with Clotilde, which made Edward's confidence escape like a slow leak in an inflatable raft. Very soon, he could be sinking.

Clotilde readily engaged him. "Hi! It's going great!" As far as Edward could tell, she had the same level of enthusiasm, if not more, than she just had with him. Edward couldn't differentiate between her responses and reactions.

"Do you guys need more time?" the server looked back and forth between them.

"Well, you can guess what I'll have. But Edward, do you know what you want?" Edward was too overwhelmed with the analysis of what she just said to Adonis to pay attention to anything else.

"Uhh..." was all Edward could muster as he scanned the list again.

The server looked at Clotilde, "You want the dark, I'm guessing?" Edward wondered why he would say it like that.

"Yes, please," Clotilde replied. The waiter looked at Edward, "She's very predictable. Always the same."

Edward lost all ability to make small-talk. He was virtually brain-dead. "Ah," was all he got out.

"And you? Do you need any help?" He asked Edward. Boy, did Edward need help, a life preserver, oxygen, brain transplant, and possibly a defibrillator for starters.

"Uhhh, do you have anything in the amber ale variety?" Edward managed to get that out coherently.

"Oh, you like your beer like you like your women, eh?" He laughed flirtatiously at Clotilde.

"My *women*? It's not exactly plural. But sure, bring me your best auburn lass in a glass." and *Bam!* The articulate and charismatic Edward was back!

"Right on." The server spun around to fetch their drinks and Clotilde chuckled. It was a great save on Edward's part, although he was still a bit perturbed.

"So, *'Chloë'*, do you come here often?" Edward asked sarcastically.

"Ugh, I know!" She rolled her eyes. "That guy cannot get my name right. Don't you hate that?"

"Yes, I totally do. I have a co-worker— a little Vespa of a co-worker— who calls me everything but Edward! She makes me crazy. And the thing is, she's a frikkin' genius, but she can't get my name right!"

Edward was thrilled to have someone to commiserate with and also relieved that Clotilde was irritated by the server getting her name wrong. She hid it very well, and that both scared and impressed Edward.

Clotilde felt the need to explain further, "A lot of us from the hospital come here; those who live around here anyway. That's why he knows me. I'm usually with the girls from work."

Edward was delighted. He was far too insecure about having to think about competition as well as just being interesting enough on his own. He found himself gazing at her again. "Um, could I say something?"

"Sure."

"I don't want to be inappropriate. You know, how they say, now, you can't say things about people's appearance, you know, because it's like— harassment, or whatever. Right?"

"Yeah, I think that's mostly a work thing, though," Clotilde replied.

"Oh. Oh, really? I just didn't want you to think I was some kind of pervert, commenting on your looks." Edward was losing ground again.

"You were commenting on my looks?" Clotilde teased but Edward didn't catch on.

"Not yet. I was going to." Edward cleared his throat awkwardly, "You are looking exceptionally, um, like extremely— but not too much," he just couldn't get it out.

The server appeared with the drinks. "Do you want food menus?"

Edward wanted to crawl under the table and Clotilde was ready to burst from sheer amusement.

"We're good for the moment, thanks," She said to the waiter, trying very hard to contain herself.

"Go on, Edward, I'm looking extremely, but not too much..." as she gestured for him to fill in the blank.

Edward wanted to start over. "Pretty. Really, really, very pretty and lovely, in fact." He threw both hands up as if to say, 'whatever'. There it was the white towel of surrender. He smiled and sipped his beer, "Cheers, Chloë!"

Clotilde laughed heartily, "Thank you, that was a very nice compliment, but you're supposed to clink my glass first before you sip yours."

"Sorry, Chloë, I needed that beer more than you." He sipped again.

Brimming with glee, Clotilde said, "Stop calling me Chloë!"

Edward took another sip, "Sorry, Chloë, no can do. It's stuck now, thanks to muscle mania over there."

Clotilde was giggling so hard she couldn't purse her lips enough to make a proper seal on the glass to take a sip without the beer running down her chin.

"Ow!" Exclaimed Edward. "Did you just kick my shin?" He was delighted.

"So what if I did?"

"Oh, man, I'm so gonna tell!"

"Who are you gonna tell?"

"Your boss! Doctor, whatshisface there. Chloë's hitting patients, and then they have to go to the ER. It's like she's an ambulance chaser or something. She's making patients for the hospital."

Edward was on a roll. He only ever had this type of rapport with Daniel. Clotilde was like the perfect woman, a female version of his best friend, only better looking and minus the neurosis.

"OK, ok, we'll call it a truce as long as you promise to stop calling me Chloë."

"Sure. But so far, I've promised you two things, and you promised not to punch me in the eye. Not that I'm keeping track, but I kind of am. What else are you going to promise me?"

Clotilde looked at Edward with purposely very dreamy eyes, and said softly, "I promise... to never kick you again."

Edward almost spit his beer out with laughter. "Deal."

Clotilde was as taken with Edward as he was with her. "Deal."

"...And, you promise to bandage me up and stuff so long as I don't come to the ER; I just seem to be a little more accident-prone than usual." The beer was quickly getting to Edward. He hadn't eaten since that starchy lunch seven hours earlier.

Clotilde promised. But now the scales were tipping the other way again. "3-2," she said. Edward clinked her glass again. "If I were you, I'd hold out for a really good one."

CHAPTER EIGHT

As another round came, Edward discovered that he and Clotilde were remarkably congenial. She laughed at his jokes, and after the first dozen or so, Edward finally stopped questioning it. Perhaps there were *two* people out of seven billion, who genuinely liked him.

That wasn't to say that people generally *didn't* like him, they did. Edward just didn't notice any higher levels of likability. The general population paid him no mind at all. When they did have to interact with him, and if there was a follow-up poll as to what adjective they'd use to describe the sort of fellow was Edward, almost unanimously, they would reply, 'nice'.

Albeit, 'nice' wasn't 'great', 'brilliant', or 'handsome', but at least he was never labelled a jerk, mean, or considered unreliable. Other than Daniel, Clotilde was the most suitable person Edward had encountered in a very long time.

The waiter arrived with their food right in the middle of a minor laughing fit about nothing at all. They had both ordered the same burger, but Clotilde had decided to splurge on fries while Edward upgraded to a caesar salad on the side.

Edward wiped tears from his eyes with his paper napkin. He hadn't laughed this much since he and Daniel went to see his cousin do stand-up. He was no longer concerned with the waiter's familiarity and knew Clotilde only had eyes for Edward. The alcohol made Edward more accepting of the euphoric infatuation and suddenly, everything looked as if it was unfolding in slow motion.

As the lantern light reflected off of Clotilde's beer glass onto her face and lips, Edward found himself captivated by the way she glistened, how her eyes glimmered with golden stars that flashed whenever she would flutter her curly lashes. Edward silently stared in awe of her.

When Clotilde realized that Edward hadn't responded to the last thing she said, she stopped, and asked awkwardly, "What's wrong? Did I say something?"

Edward smiled, somewhat embarrassed that he missed everything she just said, and not wanting to make her feel bad or have her think he was not paying attention. He was paying far too much attention to hear the words; instead, he focused on the way the words emanated through her.

"Uh... sorry. I was just looking at you." It was honest. Edward cleared his throat and began to organize his cutlery. Then in a more serious tone, he glanced up, "Could I ask you a very personal question?"

Taken aback as if playtime was abruptly over, Clotilde also became serious, "Yes, by all means."

Three whole seconds passed, and Edward managed to keep a very straight face. "How do you feel about," he began.

"Yes...?" Clotilde urged him on.

"About... people taking food from your plate?" Edward's eyes sparkled with mischief.

Clearly relieved, Clotilde dove in, "What do you mean, 'people'? Like random people walking by, or like specific people at this table?" She laughed.

"Specific people at this table," Edward stated, grinning.

"What, are you sorry you ordered that salad?"

"Maybe. I just want to try one fry to see if I made the right decision." He pleaded.

Jestingly Clotilde continued, "Ah, I don't know. I mean, I'm ok with you taking food from my plate, but what if you try the fries and then you really like them? Are you going to steal *all* my fries? You take one, then two, then the next thing you know—"

"Are they *good* fries?"

"They're *amazing* fries."

Without breaking eye contact, Edward reached across the table as Clotilde turned her plate to position the fries closer to him. Edward managed to select a single fry and pop it in his mouth, never breaking the gaze.

"Wow, those *are* good."

"You can have more, you know; I can't eat all of them." Clotilde offered, sincerely.

"That's ok. I'll order some more."

"No, no, really, you can have these. I was just teasing."

"Um... I kind of have the metabolism of a gerbil, so I'll order some and eat whatever of yours that you can't finish." Edward shrugged.

Clotilde was impressed, if not even a little envious of this quality. She never had weight issues, but was always mindful of her food intake and tried to maintain balance. Conversely, although Edward resembled a praying mantis, he definitely had the metabolism of a small rodent and was thankful he had the temperament of neither.

They began eating and agreed that everything was scrumptious but rather sloppy as they went through several rounds of napkins, and yet were thoroughly delighted with the meal and the company.

Then out it came. The big question. It was inevitable that Clotilde of all people would ask, and Edward finally decided to recount the horrific misadventure.

"So what actually happened the other night? Your eye is looking much better, by the way."

"Yes, thank you. It's healing fast." Edward finished chewing a mouthful, wiped his hands on the napkin, took a sip of beer, cleared his throat, and then just went for it. It was good for Clotilde to let him talk for a while so she could catch up with her meal.

"Daniel's gonna be so pissed that you found out the story before him." Edward was even willing to let that go. He was three beers in and this is the most fun he's had with a woman in almost a decade.

Surprised, Clotilde asked, "You haven't told Daniel? Wow. This is big."

Edward shrugged, "Yeah, well, I guess I just wasn't ready to talk about it."

He sat back in his chair and pulled it in closer to the table. "OK, so Daniel tells me about this Hallowe'en party last week. 'It's gonna be so cool, and we gotta go,'" he imitated Daniel's body language. "Basically, *Daniel* wanted to go and needed *me* to go with him. Costumes aren't really my thing. I'm just not creative like that. The place was this slick nightclub and I didn't wanna show up as a cowboy."

Clotilde chuckled briefly at the thought of Edward as a cowboy but continued to watch and listen intently as she systematically and daintily devoured her burger and fries. "Ok, well, that's intriguing. So Daniel *was* there, but he doesn't know what happened?"

With one long finger swaying at Clotilde, Edward corrected her, "No, no, you're jumping ahead. You can't make assumptions. I certainly couldn't."

Edward continued to explain as he occasionally popped a fry into his mouth and took a sip of beer.

Over the previous weekend, Edward thought at length what type of costume he would wear. He scoured the internet for lists of the 'best male costume', to no avail. He even took a trip to the local pop-up Hallowe'en shop to get ideas. He perused every row, every rack, every costume, every accessory and still couldn't figure out what to be.

According to Daniel, Hallowe'en was a time to dress up as your alter ego or your idol, or wear something that you never would. He also informed Edward that there would be attractive women there, just to keep that in mind. As if choosing a suitable costume wasn't already troublesome enough, he had the added pressure of having to make himself appealing to women!

When Edward started his search, it was no surprise that the top sellers mainly were superhero costumes. There were several problems with this. There was no guarantee that Edward would be the only "super-whoever," and quite likely, he would be the one wearing a costume that was the most ill-fitting and always too short. Spandex was out. Costumes requiring muscles were out. Manly, rugged archetypes were out. A skeleton would have been ideal were it not for the skin-tight, full-length, black bodysuit part.

Pale and pasty, he did naturally, and vampires were too sophisticated. Daniel had checked in with Edward on the weekend.

"Any luck, Edward?" He asked eagerly.

"None," Edward replied flatly. "What are you going as?" Hoping it would provide some insight.

"Moses."

"Moses? Like, biblical Moses?"

"Is there any other kind?"

"Isn't that a bit...?"

"Obvious?"

"I was going to say, sacrilegious?"

"Nowhere does it say we can't *dress up* as a prophet. Anyway, I can always say I'm Charleton Heston if anyone has a problem with it."

"Where did you get the costume?"

"My cousin was him in his high school play. Believe it or not, they did the Ten Commandments, and managed to whittle it down to an hour-and-a-half, musical."

"A musical? That's *gotta* be sacrilegious!"

"Nah, not at all. It totally sucked, but everyone was ok with it."

Edward was both baffled and intrigued by this. It barely bothered him that Daniel put absolutely no thought into his costume, a feat he would have loved to pull off himself. The idea of a musical Moses was inspiring. This was right up Edward's alley. *Satire*. That he could do.

Then seemingly out of nowhere, as if all Edward needed, was to know that it was perfectly fine to push the boundaries on Hallowe'en.

And there it was that the idea of Goth Jesus was born! What a hilarious pair they would be; Musical Moses and Goth Jesus! It would be a great conversation starter, and there was a good chance women (at least, some women) would admire the cleverness of it.

Edward began looking forward to the party and returned to the Hallowe'en shop to seek out the various parts that he knew he saw there. He had sandals at home. He just needed the shepherd's costume, fake beard, the black nail polish, the makeup, temporary spray-in hair colour, and a few fetishy looking vampire accessories and he was done.

It was magnificent!

Riveted, Clotilde was still working on her second beer, but Edward was getting a fourth. He had nothing to lose now. She was either going to accept him, or she wasn't, and Edward had just enough alcohol in him to not be concerned with negative eventualities.

As Edward wrapped up his workday on Wednesday, quite like he did every day, he planned to go home, have a quick supper, get ready for the party, meet up with Daniel and show up together. The evening started off well enough, but events unfolded differently than how Edward expected. Daniel was on his phone as they left work, more preoccupied than usual, and so they didn't leave together.

Edward was fine; he had a schedule and he was sticking to it despite leaving Daniel in the office lobby. Daniel, engrossed in his phone conversation, gestured a series of exaggerated signs, indicating that he'd text him later when he was ready.

Notwithstanding, being dressed up at a Hallowe'en party with strangers was an environment in which Edward was utterly out of his element, probably only second to being on stage in a male strip joint, he was advancing with incongruous expectancy. Upon his arrival at home, he went through the usual motions, except for the brief interruption when he laid out his costume in between preparing his boxed mac and cheese and eating it.

He reasoned that it was best to get fully dressed and then apply the black lacquer to his nails so that he could sit and wait while it dried without disturbing anything. Clotilde was notably impressed with Edward's conclusion, being that it was the first time he had ever applied nail polish.

Edward shovelled in his extra peppery mac and cheese and found it strange that he hadn't yet heard from Daniel.

He sent Daniel a quick text: "Yo, Moses. Whaddup?" he typed, jokingly, very Daniel-esque.

The only reply was, "Call you in a bit," which was not very Daniel-esque at all. Edward continued to get ready.

Everything went according to plan. Watching a nature show about lemurs, Edward believed himself to be flawlessly dressed as Goth

Jesus, outstretched on his sofa, waiting for his nails to dry. Daniel called. Immediately, Edward felt something was askew.

"Hey, Daniel."

"You're not gonna believe this."

"What? Don't back out of this."

"I can't go."

"You can't back out of this *now*!"

"Dude, I can't go!"

"What do you mean, you can't go? It was all your idea."

"I know. I know! I told my sister I'd help them out because it was Hallowe'en, but I don't remember saying it!"

"Geez, man! How could you forget that?"

"It was like at Father's Day or something. Like months ago. I don't remember at all, but my whole family will be totally vexed if I bail."

"Who can I go with? It's so last minute. I have this costume..."

"Dude, I'm sorry. It's either you're mad at me or my mother and sisters. I didn't think you wanted to go that much anyway."

"I didn't. But I'm dressed now."

Daniel continued to apologize profusely until Edward let him off the hook. Edward sat on the sofa staring at his black toenails. Nestled up beside him, Sparky offered up a comforting expression.

It was at that moment that Edward decided to behave entirely out of character. Never in his life did Edward so much as go to a bar on his own, let alone go solo to a party in a club with strangers. But it was that feeling of being Edward's alter ego that overtook him. Not that Goth Jesus was truly his alter ego, it was still a shocking contrast to Edward, the unnoticeable geek who sat at a computer all day.

"Sparky, I'm going out!" Edward slapped his leg and stood up. Sparky ran and hid. That should have been a sign. Cats tend to know things.

Edward waddled across the living room on his heels, unsure of the condition of his toenails. It had been half an hour, ample time for them to dry, but he didn't know that. He gingerly put on his sandals and checked his costume in the mirror. Edward felt it was spectacular and looked like it was constructed by someone who was regularly creative, not just accidentally so.

He left the apartment on his own, awaiting whatever life was going to throw at him. *How bad could it be?* He asked himself. For future reference, Edward made a note never to tempt fate with such questions. How could he have known that what life was going to throw at him was attached to a merciless right hook?

Had he known, he would not have gone. Had he stayed home, nothing would have changed.

At this point in Edward's story, Clotilde had finished everything she had in front of her and Edward was halfway through his beer.

So as not to monopolize the conversation, Edward asked conscientiously, "Do you want anything else? Should we go?"

Clotilde always spoke with the sound of a smile in her voice. "No, I'm good. You can finish your beer, and then if you want, we can go somewhere else. I'm very intrigued by your story. I know what my dad would say about your costume."

"Oh? Would he not approve?"

"He would totally approve! *C'est génial!* That's what he'd say." Clotilde grinned, fully appreciative of her father's potential reaction.

"That's a relief. I thought it was particularly brilliant myself, at first." Edward took a long gulp of his beer and motioned to the server to bring the bill. Clotilde reached for her purse.

"Put that away, please." Edward looked at her firmly, which was a new thing. Of course, he would usually offer, but it was very new indeed to do it with such conviction.

Clotilde politely and gratefully obliged. "Thank you. That's very sweet of you."

Mr. Muscles brought the bill over with the mobile debit machine and Edward was ready with his card.

"Was everything to your liking?" he asked Edward, making the same charming expression that he made earlier to Clotilde.

Without looking up from the machine, Edward tapped away and replied, "Yes, very much." He didn't notice the glance that the server gave to Clotilde, which was followed by a wink. It was as if to say the waiter acknowledged that Edward liked her, as well as the dinner and drinks. Edward gave him a good tip; he needed him to be on his side.

They wrapped up with a round of 'thank-you's and 'good evenings' and their pre-winter attire was donned for exiting.

The air was sharp, although still. It wasn't strolling weather. Before they headed too far in any given direction or felt too cold, Clotilde asked, "Where do you want to go?"

Edward didn't want to be presumptuous at all. He couldn't. He suggested, "We could look on our phones and see what's nearby. What do you feel like?"

Clotilde stood with her hands in her pockets while Edward floundered around his pockets, attempting to retrieve his phone. "Who lives closest?" She asked. It flew right over Edward's head.

"Who? Closest to where?" Edward continued to fiddle with his phone. "What's near me," he said aloud as he typed it.

"I mean, it's cold. We could always get a bottle of wine or something and then go to either of our places." She waited patiently for Edward to clue in.

"Well, there's a coffee shop, but it's closed. There's another pub, just over there." Edward pointed off to his right but stopped suddenly, and as he caught a glimpse of Clotilde not looking where he was pointing.

"Oh, you wanted wine? You want to go home." Edward wasn't fully clued in, but he was closer.

"Well, unless you've had too much for tonight. I mean you had four beers." She grinned square on up into his face. "I thought we could have wine together, but if you prefer coffee, that's ok too."

Edward stared blankly at her. All his newfound confidence puddled on the sidewalk. "You want to have wine or coffee together?"

"Sure, if you want to? I want to hear the rest of the story and like you, I got nothing better to do."

"Ahh, now you're mocking me. Sorry, I was a little flustered when you called me earlier." Bashfully, Edward warmed up again. Clotilde laughed heartily.

"Well, you know, I almost rescinded my offer at that point. But you're so cute, and I figured what the heck."

"Cute?" Edward could not hide his smile, although he tried. "I think *you* may need to get your eyes checked, there, lady."

"No, it's true!" Clotilde tried to convince him but she was still laughing.

"Ha! To think I let you examine my eye. I think—"

"You think what? That it's a good idea. We should get what, coffee or wine?" Clotilde was brimming with giggles.

"I think you might be a tad tipsy, my dear. But if you think we should pick-up something, you can come to my place although I have to warn you, it's extremely messy. Like extremely, extremely messy."

Edward was getting cold too and really didn't care too much as long as he was back indoors soon. He was in disbelief that not only did Clotilde think he was cute, which nobody did since he was a child, truthfully, but she also wanted to spend more time with him. At his place, or her place, whichever was closest.

"I'm not really tipsy; I just feel a little more relaxed." Clotilde felt the need to clarify. "How come you're not tipsy?"

Edward shrugged. Clotilde lead him towards a private liquor store that was open late. At Clotilde's urging, Edward continued with his story.

The Goth Jesus made his way to the club that fateful Hallowe'en night, shoving his money directly into his pocket so he could leave his wallet at home. He approached the entrance where he was met with a bouncer, at least two-and-a-half-Edwards wide and three-quarters of an Edward tall. He directed Edward where to go with a nod.

There was a short queue to pay a cover charge, which Edward did in exchange for a fluorescent pumpkin stamp on his hand. The girl at the door thought Edward was with the three people ahead of him, but as soon as he entered the central area of the nightclub, it was evident that he was alone.

Edward felt awkward but less unpleasant than he had grown accustomed to in similar situations. He was in disguise and that allowed for some anonymity. He made his way to the slick black curved bar where the cowboy bartender was chatting up some girls who looked like they were a coven of super-heroes whose costumes had shrunken in the laundry.

Being as tall as he was, it did afford Edward some attention. Now, dressed as he was with black eyeliner and all, the bartender took notice of him rather speedily. "What'll you have?" he asked just as

Edward sat on the nearest stool to the three extroverted women. He was particularly relieved that he hadn't opted for a cowboy costume.

"Whatever they're having. Looks like fun." Edward said cheerily and politely, in sharp contradiction to his translucent facade. The bartender was visibly taken aback by the contrast, but obliged cordially and placed a fourth 'witch's brew' on the bar. One of the girls turned to look at Edward, as none of them had noticed him until now, and let out an exaggerated synthetic giggle. It confused Edward. It was obviously a well-rehearsed melody, and yet she almost appeared flirtatious. Well, it was somewhere between flirtatious and mockery, which was why Edward decided to look elsewhere.

He sipped his drink pensively as he tried to pinpoint the various flavours within it. He placed it back on the bar and slowly spun around on the fixed stool to scan the decorations and the costumes of the people who were trickling into the place. With his back partially to the bar and partially to the girls, Edward suddenly kept getting bumped in the back. He moved forward on the seat as much as he could, but there was a guy dressed as a surfer who had wedged himself between Edward and Super Girl.

As much as Edward was non-confrontational, this blowhard who pushed up against his back repeatedly so that he could relentlessly hit on the young woman began to ruffle Edward's feathers. Edward turned back to the bar, hoping to squeeze past him. Edward sipped his drink while listening to one cheesy line after the other. The surfer bragged non-stop, but the girl was having none of it.

"You're very beautiful," the surfer told her.

"Thanks," replied the woman, dryly.

Even Edward could tell she wanted to end the conversation. Then, as the surfer attempted to puff up his chest even further, he accidentally elbowed Edward in the kidney. As a knee-jerk reaction, Edward jumped. The surfer turned around and rather than apologize, sneered at Edward, "Hey buddy, why don't you move down a bit. It's pretty tight over here." Then muttered under his breath, "asshole".

Edward grabbed his drink and slurped it furiously as he stared at the back of the guy's head, then moved over two seats. It wasn't far enough; he could still hear the guy bragging about his job, his promotion, his car, and his bench presses. It made Edward feel uneasy.

Edward turned to see if Super Girl actually looked like she was impressed with his monologue, but she appeared neutral at best. The surfer noticed her glance over to Edward and decided this was the reason for her not being fully enraptured by his nauseating credentials.

"What are you looking at, asshole?" He aggressively began to bully Edward.

Edward felt sick to his stomach and was suddenly woozy. "Uhh…" was all he could muster.

"Uhhhh??" mimicked the surfer. He turned around fully to face Edward. "What are you supposed to be anyway?" His two friends quickly flanked him. One was in a karate robe over his jeans and the other was a ninja.

Edward cleared his throat. He instantaneously regretted his decision to get dressed up for Hallowe'en. "Uh… Goth Jesus," Edward mumbled. He couldn't see straight and decided that perhaps he should just excuse himself and leave as quickly as possible.

But it was too late for that. "Goth *Jesus*?" The three guys encroached on Edward and looked him up and down. "Do you think that's *funny*?" shouted the ninja. Then the karate kid chimed in, "Maybe he thinks it's clever," roared the ninja.

Then, Edward stood up, hoping to make his get-away. He was timorous and light-headed, "I did, yes. I'm so, so, sorry to think it was clever and also funny. I truly did." Edward slurred his words, but the trio thought he was just trying to be a smart-ass. Not wanting to appear intimidated by Edward's height, they collectively interpreted his standing-up as a threat.

The three women started to back away and headed for the side exit. This displeased the surfer, who turned back to call to Super Girl when Edward interrupted him, and in a very drunken manner, swaying like a reed in a gale, said, "Oh let her go, geez! She was in *agony* listening to your boring diatri— dia, dianthrive, whatever thing." And with that, the surfer's rage-meter hit its maximum. He swung up at Edward and toppled him back towards the bar.

After that, although parts of it unravelled in slow motion for Edward, everything escalated rapidly. Before he knew it, Edward was flung outside with the three guys. He floundered, punches were thrown about like confetti, a few kicks got in as well, and he was pleasantly surprised that the karate kid and the ninja were total frauds. It all became a blur, and Edward picked himself up off the concrete as the crowd looked on keenly. Except for the brief stop to get a mickey of bourbon, Edward waddled home, bewildered.

After hearing the tale, Clotilde was shocked. They approached Edward's apartment building and he felt a great deal of relief to have finally told someone.

"That could have been so much worse!" Clotilde declared as they got into the elevator. "You didn't want to go straight to the hospital or press charges?" She asked again, knowing the whole story now. "I mean, they ganged up on you and punched you and assaulted you for no reason."

Edward was glad to have gotten the information off his chest and even more satisfied to have Clotilde's sympathy. But he confirmed, "Well, what was I going to say in that state? I felt humiliated more than anything. Not to mention the costume and everything." Edward admitted.

"Would you be able to identify them if you saw them again?" Clotilde questioned.

"Well, not the ninja whatsoever but the karate guy, probably. However, I'd be able to identify the main guy with my eyes closed! I saw his face, with sunglasses on, mind you. But ugh, his voice - he blathered on and on about himself forever." Edward shuddered.

Edward had been adequately distracted until the moment he unlocked the door to his suite. A real live woman was about to enter his home. She wasn't a relative or delivery person, and he felt an hour's worth of frantic stress rush up his neck to flood his face with visible warmth. He paused with his hand on the doorknob.

"Are you sure you want to come in?" Edward turned back to Clotilde as a last-ditch effort to allow her an 'out' in case she had changed her mind. She looked at him soberly and slightly rejected, "Do you *not want* me to come in?" She whispered with a noticeable quiver in her voice.

"I do— absolutely. Just checking that *you* want to come in. This isn't a regular thing for me and to be perfectly honest," Edward let out a deep, vulnerable sigh, "you're the first date who's been here."

"How long have you lived here?"

"Seven years," blurted Edward before Clotilde even finished her last syllable.

"Open the door." Clotilde wasn't one to prolong the inevitable.

"OK." Edward walked in and held the door open for Clotilde, who closed it and assertively, locked it behind her.

CHAPTER NINE

It was almost 11 pm, and Sparky was very keen to be up tricking a new person into playing with him while simultaneously snaffling some affection. Clotilde scanned the room, intrigued; Edward fussed about the mess and apologized about his ineptitude with interior décor.

Sparky's meows crescendoed until Edward took notice of him. Breathlessly he introduced the feline, "and this annoying creature is Sparky, my roommate." Edward took Clotilde's coat and placed it over the slightly worn armchair because he wouldn't dare open the hall closet, which was desperately overflowing with an array of useless items that either needed to be organized or thrown away altogether.

"Hello, Sparky," murmured Clotilde in a velvety voice as she squatted down to pet Sparky and scratch him under his chin. Sparky started to purr and casually peered out of one eye at Edward in his typical mocking fashion. Not that it was a competition, but it appeared that Sparky was getting much more physical attention from Clotilde than Edward did all night.

"Ok, ok, Sparky, stop flirting with the guest." Edward needed to interrupt this love fest. Clotilde giggled, "Cats sure know how to train us, don't they?"

"Sure do. I'm convinced he knows more than me about pretty much everything. If only he had opposable thumbs. Eh, Sparky?" Edward glared at Sparky, clearly broadcasting psychically to leave Clotilde alone. Sparky ignored Edward, as was his nature.

As if Edward couldn't feel any more uncomfortable and in unfamiliar territory than he had all evening, he was now feeling particularly self-conscious. He became aware of his every movement, his habits and patterns with regard to how he traveled through his private space and even felt like he was in someone else's body, living someone else's life.

From Edward's perspective, Clotilde didn't appear nervous, although she was. Edward stood halfway between the living room and kitchen, in the middle of no man's land, holding the brown paper bag enveloping the bottle of wine. Clotilde stood awkwardly at the far end of the living room with an ocean of furniture and various remote controls strewn between them. Edward was losing ground again.

"Shall I go open this, then?" Edward asked, raising the bag of wine.

"It would be easier to drink, that way," joked Clotilde as she zigzagged through the obstacles attempting to bridge the gap between them. Her seeming ease with quick replies impressed Edward because he often thought of ideal responses hours after an incident had passed, or made witty comments entirely by accident. It was sometimes hard for him to tell if people were laughing at him or with him.

They made their way to the kitchen, and even Sparky sprung to the counter to watch his master crumble. Edward impatiently rummaged around the kitchen utensil drawer as he grew increasingly frustrated.

"What are you looking for?" asked Clotilde.

"The corkscrew thingy," mumbled Edward, as he stood bent in half, face-first into the drawer, clanking around its contents.

Clotilde delicately slipped the bottle up out of the bag. "Uh, I think it's a screw top." She grinned.

Edward continued to rummage for a moment before realizing what she had said. "What?"

Clotilde lifted the neck of the bottle up again and then completely out of the bag, unscrewed the cap and said, "Voilà! No tools needed, just a couple of glasses."

Edward sheepishly slid the drawer closed. "Glasses. Right. I think I might have two wine glasses, but there's a very good chance they won't match."

"That's not a problem." Clotilde smiled, quite aware that she was visiting an authentic bachelor pad.

Sparky looked on condescendingly while Edward opened and closed cupboard doors. "You see, I usually just use a couple of regular glasses for water and smoothies and stuff, and I drink beer out of the bottle so..." Finally, he found two glasses. One looked more like a water goblet, slightly tinted smokey blue, and the other had a shorter stem with raised swirls around the bowl. He presented them to Clotilde so she could choose which she preferred.

Grinning, Clotilde had a serious selection to make. "Swirls or smokey?" Edward asked.

"Well, 'swirls' seem a little more me. I'll take this one." She said. But Edward suddenly started to question himself as he attempted to estimate equal amounts of wine in both glasses silently. Why and when did he acquire these swirly girly wine glasses? Were they already in the apartment? Were they from his university days? Did he buy them himself? He couldn't remember.

Noticing his solemn expression, Clotilde had to ask, "You look very serious; everything ok?"

"Yes, I just can't figure out for the life of me, where the hell these glasses came from?"

Clotilde started to laugh and having just taken a small sip of wine, also began to choke and regretfully, snort. She was mortified and couldn't stop any part of it.

Edward, not realizing that Clotilde might be embarrassed, began to panic and proceeded to slap her on the back as was the custom since childhood. Of course, this made Clotilde cough more and laugh harder, and before Edward could hit her again, she waved her hands in surrender which was the universally understood signal that he must stop.

After clearing her throat, and wiping her eyes, Clotilde said, "Sorry, I feel so stupid. I wouldn't have taken a sip right then if I knew you were going to make me laugh!" Edward reached over and grabbed a tissue for her. He was very confused. It wasn't his modus operandi to make girls laugh, not to mention, this was one of those times when he didn't know that he had even said anything remotely amusing.

To avoid any further confusion or embarrassment, Edward suggested they go back to the living room, and see if there was a movie they could watch. Clotilde carried her glass, and Edward carried his glass and the bottle. As they sat down on the sofa like a pair of synchronized swimmers, perfectly timed and moving in unison, Clotilde asked, "Are we gonna watch 'Netflix and chill'?"

Edward wasn't sure what she was asking, so he blinked a couple of times as if to reboot his internal hard drive. "Do you mean that literally? Because," he cleared his throat nervously before he continued, "I believe it's also a euphemism. A euphemism for, you know." he tried to be polite and didn't want to be overhasty.

Clotilde's eyes widened as she realized what Edward was describing and what she had inadvertently said. "Oh! God, no!" She tried to make it clear that was not what she was insinuating, but by doing so, it almost made it sound like an impossibility. A horrified expression came over Edward's face.

"No, I didn't mean it like that!"

"Like what? We can watch *actual* Netflix, which is what I thought you meant."

"Okay, phew! Yeah, I didn't mean the uh, euphemism, thing. Not that that's a *bad* thing. I just didn't want you to think I was suggesting that when I wasn't. Suggesting it. At this moment."

It took a while, but Edward was finally able to recognize that Clotilde was fumbling with words as much as he usually did. On the inside, he was delighted. On the outside, he kept up the pretence and watched her flounder.

"What would you like to watch?" Edward turned to the variety of remotes laid out on the ottoman and started clicking away, turning on the streaming components, switching his TV's HDMI input, and yet another clicker for the surround sound. Clotilde held her breath in silence.

"Do you like Sci-fi?" He asked pleasantly. Clotilde let out her breath and a good half of her tension. "I love Sci-fi." She said.

With a twinkle in his eye, Edward asked, "Have you ever seen the original, _The Day The Earth Stood Still?_"

Elated, Clotilde replied, "No! Do you have it?" Of course, Edward had it. He was happy to impress her with something, even if it was just a mere digital trinket. Clotilde was just pleased that she wasn't choking, spewing wine out her nose, or making inappropriate innuendo. Edward was happy that he wasn't either.

Edward poured himself another glass of wine, dimmed the lamp, then sat closer to Clotilde, to which she responded by moving a little closer to him as well. They were both slightly a flutter but continued to look straight ahead as the film began when Edward mumbled, "You almost sounded repulsed by the idea of the euphemism."

Sweetly, Clotilde whispered, "Sorry, I didn't mean that."

"Didn't mean which part?" Whispered Edward.

"I'm not at all repulsed by the idea of the euphemism 'Netflix and chill', I just meant it literally in this case."

The opening scenes showed up on the giant flat-screen TV.

"Not repulsed in general, or with me, specifically?" It must have been all the alcohol keeping Edward's inhibitions at bay.

Clotilde turned towards the side of Edward's face, "You, specifically. I find you as far away from repulsive as one could get."

Edward turned to face Clotilde. They were mere inches apart.

"You know, that's one of the nicest things any person of the opposite sex has ever said to me," Edward stated honestly.

Clotilde thought he was mocking her and started to laugh because it still sounded awful. "Not repulsive at all." He continued. Clotilde started to gently slap his arm, "Stop it!" She laughed again. "I want to watch the movie!"

"I think I'm going to have that on my epitaph, 'here lies Edward, who was not repulsive at all.'" He could barely get the words out, as he was laughing too.

The giggling got out of hand, as it sometimes did between close friends or those who share similar sensibilities. Sometimes for no reason, not because something was exceptionally funny, but when both people are overtired, giddy, or nervous in this case, desperately needing to release the tension.

"Now you're going to have to start it again. I've missed about five minutes of the movie!" Clotilde grabbed the remote and started to rewind.

Jokingly, Edward bellowed, "What!? You never, *never, ever* steal a man's remote!"

"Oh, this is a *man's* remote?" Clotilde swiped the clicker over to her far side so Edward couldn't get it. But of course, he could get it if he *wanted* to. Playfully, he attempted to reach around with his gangly arm and grab the remote back, but Clotilde tilted away from him and hid it behind her back with both hands.

Instinctively, and without a second thought, Edward flipped his left knee over his right, and straight over Clotilde's lap. He was suddenly straddling her and reached around both sides of her to grab the remote. The buttons were getting clicked and the volume on the TV was getting louder and louder, then it paused and started again, and Clotilde was roaring because Edward was tickling her. Technically speaking, although he hadn't noticed, he was hugging her, while straddling her lap, like a leggy spider wrapped around a fly.

"Ah-ha! I got it! I got it!" Shouted Edward triumphantly. Clotilde, weary from wrestling, laughing and crying, relaxed her body but did not relinquish the remote. Edward also stopped wriggling and suddenly realized where he was. They locked their muzzy gazes upon each other as best they could.

Breathlessly, Edward uttered, "You have to give it to me, now; I got it."

Clotilde waited for a hefty second and gave it to him, all right. She planted one firm kiss squarely on his lips.

Stunned, Edward felt the entire evening's alcohol content flood to his brain at once. "I feel drunk." He said. "Can you give me one of those again?" He asked because it may not have actually happened. It never happened like that before. There was a good chance it didn't happen now. It was highly likely, he imagined it. He tried to focus on Clotilde's features, which were now slightly blurred.

Clotilde leaned forward again and kissed Edward for a few seconds longer. It *was* real and it *did* happen. Edward released his grasp of the remote and rolled over to the far side of Clotilde, where he just slumped down on the sofa beside her.

"I'm suddenly *so* drunk." He announced again.

"It's about time. You had six drinks. I had two-and-a-half!" She said as she pulled the remote out from behind her back and handed it to Edward.

"Nah, you keep it." Edward fanned it away.

"You're letting me keep your remote? Wow, that was easy. One little kiss." Clotilde smiled; she was getting drowsy and Edward was stupefied. "Two kisses." He confirmed, raising two fingers like a 'V'.

They decided to save the movie for another night. There was definitely going to be another date. Neither of them had connected with anyone in such a naturally unstructured way in so long, that it was simultaneously incontestable and yet still surreal.

People would say things like, "Pinch me to see if this is real", and Edward always thought it was a stupid comment to make. He never could relate to it.

Until now.

You could have perforated him with a knitting needle, and he might not have felt it.

Clotilde left by taxi and they agreed to catch up soon. There was no third kiss or any hugs for that matter; just an awkward handshake at the door and a wave goodbye as Clotilde got in the cab. All the same, they were both enraptured.

Edward exited the elevator and walked back to his apartment, where Sparky sat waiting for him smugly.

"Oh, Sparky, Sparky, Sparky!" Edward swooned around the living room, plopped himself down on the sofa, put his feet up on the ottoman and polished off Clotilde's glass of wine while he looked for a new series to watch on Netflix.

"Sparky, *Blissed Out*, doesn't even begin to describe it!" Edward sighed and Sparky turned himself into a near-perfect circle on the middle of his lap.

CHAPTER TEN

Sparky had a knack of perching precisely on Edward's bladder most mornings, kneading his abdomen, purring and vibrating. It wasn't a food request, but Sparky knew it would always wake Edward up and he could begin conversing with someone, even a lesser being such as he was.

Saturday began in the same way, but Edward had fallen asleep on the sofa, still wearing Friday's clothes. It took him a few seconds to realize where he was and what had transpired. The TV was off. The remotes were on either side of him. There were two empty mismatched wine glasses in front of him.

Edward leaped up, giving no consideration to Sparky whose reflexes allowed him to vault safely and gracefully to the side. Edward started to pace. He traced his steps back to where he had last left his phone. It was still in his coat pocket. With minimal battery power left, he could see the time displayed on the screen was now 10:26 a.m. and that he had six unread text messages.

With everything he had to drink the previous night, it was remarkable that he managed to sleep so late without any prompting from his bladder. And with that realization, he dashed to the bathroom and tried to multitask— five messages from Daniel and one from Clotilde. Clotilde's text said, "Made it home safe. Thanks for the fun evening."

Edward ran back to his room and put the phone on the charger. Seated on the far side of the bed, he began with Daniel's quintet of messages.

9:38 PM "Pssst. Dude. RU still on the date?"

9:50 PM "Hey. How did it go? Updates would be nice."

10:16 PM "All good? Call me back. Or text w/e"

11:06 PM "Fine. Don't tell me. Either ur dead, ur phone's dead, or u got lucky."

12:12 AM "Duuuuuuude. You're killing me."

Edward could not help but be amused and considered torturing Daniel further, but instead replied with a short text. "Phone almost dead. Charging. Gonna shower. Call you after. Date was all right." Edward knew he was being a bit cheeky with the last part because Daniel would definitely read into it with his jaded, pessimistic outlook. As much as he tried to be supportive and optimistic, he was equally ready for things to fall apart completely.

Before Edward could return the phone to the side table, Daniel immediately texted back. "All right?!?!?! Scale of 1-10??"

Daniel was nothing if not predictable. It was a trait Edward relied on. "9.7" Edward texted his response and without turning back, dashed to the washroom to shower. He knew that would at least provide Daniel with some sense of relief and would tie him over until he could get all the details.

As Edward returned to the bathroom, he could hear voices coming through the hole in the ceiling. His building had gone through several era-specific remodellings over the course of its lifetime. The original construction hadn't allowed for an elevator. That was a 1970s addition. The tiles were original; many kitchen cabinets were too. Grout had been redone, and sinks and tubs had been re-enamelled in spots. There had been phases of pristinely varnished wood floors and various incarnations of wall-to-wall carpets from shag to waffle. Despite everything the building has gone through, the venting holes in the bathrooms remained.

A flirtatious giggle from a female voice echoed from the upstairs unit. It caught Edward's attention and he listened impishly. It was followed by a man's voice who sounded as though he was laughing at his own jokes. Then the woman squealed playfully. Edward couldn't help but listen to hear if he could get the gist of what they were saying.

He decided to do his eye treatment after his shower, as Mother Nature beckoned in a timely fashion nudging Edward to grab an old copy of Reader's Digest while parking himself upon the throne. He attempted reading an article about the resurgence of fly fishing but just couldn't focus, as the voices whirling through the vent were very distracting.

There was that fun-loving giggle again, followed by what seemed to Edward to be a very put-on macho-sounding bellowing laugh. It literally sounded like a booming, overly pronounced, "Ha. Ha. Ha." to which the woman would respond with ticklish giggles.

What's this? There was a third voice. Another female voice, deeper than the first, was murmuring something in a soft lustful way and laughing. Edward became so enthralled. He was extra quiet in the hopes of grasping just a snippet of what they were saying. If he could have squinted with his ears, he would have. In fact, he tried very diligently to do just that.

The male voice was cooing words that were still incomprehensible to Edward, no matter how he fine-tuned his hearing. Then the high-pitched woman's voice said something like, "That's what you always say!" followed by throaty laughter, from the other woman and humming agreement sounds by the man.

This was too much for Edward to fathom as he sat there, squinting at the ceiling and losing his place in the magazine. He had finally just had a date, with '*a*', *singular*, woman, for the first time in years, and barely managed a kiss out of the ordeal. Meanwhile, this character with his fake laugh had two women with him in the bathroom.

All of Edward's inadequacies returned. He hadn't even noticed Sparky sitting on the mat beside him, staring as if equally perplexed by the kinky mischief upstairs. Edward cleared his throat suddenly as he snapped out of his haze. The voices upstairs stopped, abruptly. *They* were now listening.

Edward mouthed to his feline companion, "*Oh my god they can hear me!!*" he whispered, horrified. He was finished what he was doing and immediately hopped up to start the shower. Edward didn't know what an auditory voyeur was called, or if there was such a thing, but he certainly didn't want people to think *he* was one!

"Act normal," he said to himself as he tested the water and entered the shower pulling the foggy plastic curtain closed. He realized the irony in this. There was nothing normal about talking to himself or telling himself to ignore the ménage-à-trois overhead. He hummed purposefully as if the rushing water wasn't enough to drown out the remnants of dialogue from upstairs.

"Just minding my own business fa-la-la-la-la-lah," Edward mumbled a tune as he rinsed all the suds from the top of his head. It was no easy feat folding himself up in such a manner as to get his head under the shower to start with.

He shook it off. He shook everything off. What type of guy lived upstairs? Had he ever seen him before? Had he seen the women? Were they all roommates? Were they attractive? Would he be able to tell if they were ménage-à-trois material? Was Clotilde that type? Did she expect Edward to be? He could barely manage an individual woman, let alone a pair of them.

The water suddenly got cool, which was a lucky break for Edward because he needed to be pulled back off the cliff of self-deprecation, on the chilly slopes of Mt.Saint Pity. He wiped his face down with his wrinkled fingers and shut off the water. He stood there for a moment. The upstairs shower was running.

"Great." Edward was relieved. They probably didn't know who he was either. He swiped the curtain open, scaring Sparky out the door with a disgruntled meow. As he started drying himself, Edward couldn't help but suspect that Clotilde would probably *not* call him back. He knew that she had texted last night and so it was probably his turn to reply, but he was still under the impression that this was a one-time event, a single show, no repeats. There was no basis for this hypothesis, but there it was, as soggy as the tattered bathmat that Edward stood upon.

Edward tidied up the bathroom somewhat and proceeded with his eye-care regimen. There was only a slight yellowing and a vague hint of purple left. The goopiness was minimal. He sighed repeatedly.

He could hear the drone of his cell phone vibrating from the bedroom. It was probably Daniel. With his soaked towel drooping around his hips, Edward sluggishly moped into the next room, shuffled around the bed, and picked up his phone.

Clotilde was calling.

Without second-guessing himself, Edward answered, "Hello?" sounding distinctly confused.

"Edward?" Asked Clotilde, chirpy but reflecting Edward's confusion.

"Yes... Hi!" Edward perked up. Genuinely and pleasantly surprised, he delicately sat down on the edge of the bed, holding his towel politely closed. He continued, "I saw your text that you reached home. This morning though, so I didn't—" he was cut off by Clotilde.

"Edward! You need to get a blood test!" she blurted out impatiently.

"What?" Edward was baffled.

"How many drinks did you have last night?"

"Why do I need a blood test?"

"OK, listen. How many drinks did you have at the Hallowe'en party?"

"Uhh... one?"

"One." Clotilde sounded excited as if she just made a discovery. "That's what I thought you said."

"Yes, I did. I had one cocktail and I—" he was cut off again.

"And how many did you have last night?"

"Well, I had four beers, my wine, and then yours," Edward admitted.

"Yeah, exactly. Four large beers, wine and you weren't drunk."

"No, not really."

"Not at all. And the night you were at the party? How drunk were you?" Clotilde asked exuberantly.

"Oh, man, I was totally shit-faced." He didn't mean to say it that way, but he couldn't retract it with Clotilde talking so fast.

"On *one* cocktail?" There was a huge 'ah-ha' tone to Clotilde's statement. "You didn't think that was weird?"

"Well, the shit-kicking portion of the evening kind of over-shadowed everything..." He said 'shit' again, nervously. "But now that you mention it. Yeah. Whoa! *Wait a minute.*" Edward slowly stood up, realizing Clotilde was on to something, but not sure exactly what.

"Edward, if you were given Rohypnol, we need to do a urine test immediately to see if you have any traces left."

Edward's mouth gaped open just as his towel slid off. He didn't react to it at all. Naked and pale, he asked, "But who would give me... isn't that the date rape drug?" He was primarily bewildered, while in the background of his psyche, there was a hint of contentment creeping in because Clotilde seemed to care about him, at least in as much as a medical practitioner would.

"Maybe it wasn't meant for *you*!"

Edward's mind was whizzing around playing the scenes from that night backwards and forwards at blistering speed.

Clotilde urged Edward to get ready as quickly as possible and meet her at the blood lab next to the clinic. Edward had barely enough time to imagine that there would be a second meeting with Clotilde, let alone one so soon after their date. But this wasn't a date, and Edward reminded himself of this fact over twenty-seven times, while on his way over to the lab.

As Edward ran, hopped on and off curbs, jumped and scuttled between fellow pedestrians, checked his phone, he received a text from Daniel, asking for some sign of life, to which Edward responded with a callback.

Daniel answered on the first ring, "Dude! For god's sake! I'm dying here. Finally! Tell me everything."

"Yeah, hello to you too."

"Where are you and why do you sound out of breath?"

"Dude, you're not going to believe this. I'm on my way to the lab to get a urine test for Rohypnol!" Edward gave Daniel the most recent status update first.

"What?! You think Clotilde—" Daniel shouted, half delighted it seemed to Edward.

Edward entered the lab and spotted Clotilde. "No, not Clotilde; don't be ridiculous. I gotta go. I'm here now." He tried to mumble the few words with his lips almost closed.

Clotilde swung around from the counter. She still looked radiant and not at all tired. Edward was speechless as she gestured for him to approach quickly.

"This is my friend," Clotilde nodded to the nurse behind the counter. "She just needs you to sign this, and they'll do it right away." She handed Edward a form.

There were so many things Edward wanted to talk to Clotilde about. But, he was inexplicably and softly enraptured by her, even more so than yesterday. He signed the form, and the other nurse handed him a sealed plastic jar. "Give me your sample in this, and then we'll do the test."

She pointed to the sign on her left, indicating where the washrooms were. Edward looked at Clotilde, who urged him to go quickly.

"It's been two-and-a-half days, but they can usually detect it even seventy-two hours after."

Clotilde looked at him so kindly; Edward was willing to provide her with a sample of just about anything she asked for. She could tell he was enamoured as he looked at her all dreamy-eyed. "Go, pee already." Smiling, she pushed him towards the door. "You can stare at me when you're done."

Embarrassed for being so obvious, Edward pushed the door open and felt awkward again. This was usual. He wasn't aware he had been staring at Clotilde, but obviously, she didn't mind. This was *not* usual. He tried urinating into the cup, still relatively confused about everything going on.

He wasn't sure how much to put in the container, so he filled it and tightened the lid securely. Edward washed his hands, cleaned the container, and dried it with a paper towel. He decided that maybe it was a good idea to wrap it in another paper towel so as not to have it exposed or to have the nurse have direct contact with it, just to be considerate.

Clotilde waited impatiently for him in the foyer. "Come on," she hurried him as she was about to take the cup from him. Edward turned it away.

"OK, you don't want me to hold the sample." Clotilde laughed and raised both hands defensively.

"Yeah, there's no need to get in contact with any." Edward insisted as he handed it to the other nurse who had gloves on.

She took it from Edward, "Wow, that's a huge sample." She nodded to Clotilde and then went to the back. A few people in the waiting room looked up and smirked.

Jokingly, Edward responded with a bit of forethought, "Oh, there's a lot more where that came from, baby!" and immediately felt himself blush with embarrassment.

Clotilde giggled and leaned in to whispered to Edward sweetly, "I'm sure, but they usually only need a couple of millilitres." and then suggested, "Let's get a coffee and come back."

Edward followed along in agreement but had to ask, "So how did you come to this? I'm so blown away. I fell asleep on the couch, and I woke up all wonky. My phone was dead; I was still dressed, I took a shower - oh wait 'til I tell you about that!" He laughed in disbelief at first, as if he was talking to Daniel. Then he remembered what he was thinking before and that maybe Clotilde was more like them and less like Edward. Suddenly his face became solemn again.

"What? In the shower?" Clotilde was amused.

"No, no, my neighbours. It's nothing. Another time." Edward waved his hands around as if to erase the air where he let out those words. "Tell me how you came to this conclusion." He redirected the conversation once again.

There was a small coffee stand in the cafeteria of the building. Edward poured two coffees and paid for them while Clotilde carried them to the area where the cream and sugar were laid out.

As they stirred the cream in their coffees and secured the lids, Clotilde explained. "Sometimes, my brain just solves shit on its own." She said it now. Edward didn't feel so bad. "It's like I hear all the info, but then my brain solves the problem if there is one. Then I wake up, boom! There's the answer!"

Edward was impressed because a similar thing would happen to him. "Oh wow! That happens to me at work. I'm sitting there, and something isn't jiving. I leave it, and at night my brain dreams of how to fix a line of code or figures out *which* line of code needs fixing. So I get it."

Clotilde was equally impressed with Edward. "Cool. I was thinking about how much you drank, and nothing changed. So when you told me what happened at the club with the obnoxious guy and that you just had that one drink and got so wasted, I thought something was up."

"Are you saying that the guy who beat me up, slipped me the drug?"

"I think he meant to give it to the girl he was chatting up!"

Edward's eyes opened as wide as possible. Clotilde mimicked him. "You're mocking me again." He said and then sipped his coffee.

"Let's not start that again! I laughed myself to sleep thinking about you and that remote!"

Edward was stupefied. It almost sounded as if Clotilde still liked him. He was blissfully shocked.

They sat anxiously in the lab until the nurse emerged from a back cubicle. She waved at Clotilde, motioning for them to come around to a small office.

"Tilly told me what happened." She said to Edward while looking at Clotilde and continued, "And it looks like the test is positive for Flunitrazepam, which is basically the same thing, as you suspected. You might have some amnesia effects or felt like you had a bad hangover. Sometimes people totally pass out and don't recall being sexually assaulted. But you're very lucky in a way."

"Yeah, well, I wasn't sexually assaulted for one." Edward just wanted to clarify that for the record. "It was better that it was given to me instead of the girl it was likely intended for, I guess."

"I'll make you a copy of this paperwork if you plan on filing it with the police or just for your records." The nurse got up to make a photocopy.

Edward turned to Clotilde in astonishment. "Well, that's something!"

Clotilde was glad that she acted so quickly. "I know!"

"Yeah, who would have thought your nickname was *Tilly*!" Edward was delighted with himself as he caught Clotilde off-guard. She responded by elbowing him, smiling and not saying a word. Her eyes danced, and Edward began to think that it might just be real.

CHAPTER ELEVEN

The idea that Edward's world had suddenly become this portrayal of a life filled with adventure, romance, and intrigue, was so novel that he found himself uttering repeated sounds of wonderment. "Ha!" and "Wow!" he would say after prolonged moments of silence when his mind would revert to reviewing the latest events yet again.

How could everything have changed so much based on one tiny decision? Maybe it was because it *wasn't* such a minor decision, although it could be likened to nothing more than a coin-toss. Because for Edward to even get dressed up on Hallowe'en was a big deal but then attending a party at a nightclub *alone* where he knew no one, was no small thing. Prior to that moment, the decision to not stay home when Daniel couldn't make it, Edward's life carried him along. It protected him, buoyantly projected him forward, and always managed to keep him afloat, unaware of the shrouded misdeeds of the common man.

In Edward's simplicity, he was far from common. He began to wonder if he had messed with fate, or had he bypassed fate up until now? Maybe it was Daniel who threw things off course by not going with him to the party. Edward speculated what would have happened had they been there together. Perhaps they would have sat at a very different corner of the club and none of this would have transpired.

The obnoxious guy would have given an unsuspecting young lady Rohypnol and would have done god-knows-what to her; Edward most probably would not have been in a fight. Hence, he wouldn't have had a goopy eye and subsequently have had no need to go to the hospital. He wouldn't have met Clotilde, and it could have been years before he ever went on a date!

Edward was thinking himself in circles.

The concept of destiny or fate stumped Edward, and for as clever a man as he was, it made his brain throb with perplexed frustration. How could one know, or believe, that events and pathways were predetermined and that every choice was not a choice at all but previously outlined in a life's itinerary? Was it then possible to mess up destiny? Could it be avoided? Was there even an inkling that Edward would not have gone to the party?

Perhaps, Edward concluded, there was some fluidity to fate. If meeting Clotilde was destined to have happened, he might have met her no matter what. Had he not gone to the party, maybe weeks or months later, he would have met her in the pub or on the sidewalk.

But for now, this was Edward's course. He had interceded, unknowingly, on behalf of a woman in a nightclub, gotten knocked about, and met a wonderful nurse who —he dared to think— might just become his girlfriend.

In actuality, fate had been lying there dormant, waiting for Edward to push himself ever so slightly out of his comfort zone. And there, he did feel a great deal of discomfort, some of which was lingering still. But for the larger picture, he was better off. In fact, everything was better off and Edward had no idea.

"You're awfully quiet!" Clotilde spoke up and abruptly broke Edward's rhythmic neurotic internal monologue.

"Sorry!" Edward was happy to leave his thoughts for the moment. "I was just thinking about the past week and how everything is just so crazy!"

"What are you going to do about it? Do you want to file a report?" Clotilde asked.

Edward paused for an instant, "I don't know if I want to do that just yet. I mean, can they go off my description of the guy; can anybody prove he did it?"

Clotilde gave Edward's point some consideration. "Yeah, I don't know. Maybe the club has security cameras, but I don't know if they do actually go through the trouble to look into it that far."

"I'll think about it. It might just be better to file a report, and then if it ever happens again to someone else, they'll have a better case against the guy."

"Maybe they already have a case against the guy."

Edward and Clotilde raised eyebrows at each other as if they were part-time sleuths trying to solve a crime. They were surprisingly compatible and similar in their reactions and habits.

An awkward junction arose. Edward asked, "Well, I was going to head home and do some stuff, then I have to head out again later and get some groceries and things." He gestured directions at her.

Awkwardly, Clotilde chimed in, "Me too. I might take a nap, and I have to do some housecleaning and laundry and 'stuff'" She pointed vaguely in the opposite direction.

Their feet were firmly suctioned to the sidewalk, some distance from each other, as the pair pivoted from the waist, afraid to come closer or step further apart.

"Oh, but thank-you, though!" Edward hopped back into the conversation, "Thanks for your— insight! Yeah, and quick thinking. You managed to get me out of bed pretty fast there!" He laughed foolishly. "I wasn't in bed, but I was out of the house pretty fast, thanks to you."

Clotilde stood calmly as she watched Edward getting flustered. "Well, you're welcome. You're certainly very welcome." They stared at each other for another heavy second. "And I didn't mean to rush you out of bed."

"Out of the house."

"Yes."

They both painfully wanted to go for a fully sober kiss, but neither of them could make the first move with all the pendant reality suspended around them. Edward talked himself out of it with thoughts like, "Don't go for a kiss now; she might think that's rude." And Clotilde talked herself out of it by telling herself, "He's going to think you're being inappropriate right after he discovered he had been given the date-rape drug!"

Instead, Clotilde opened her arms wide to invite a big friendly hug. Edward, relieved, obliged and leaned in. They tapped each other on the back, possibly a few taps too many, while Edward did semi-accidentally attempt to kiss the air beside her cheek and kissed her ear instead. He then pulled away while Clotilde felt it fair to reciprocate but ended up just kissing nothing at all as they stared at each other with excruciating embarrassment.

"Maybe later we could do something?" Edward blurted. He just didn't want her to file him into the friend zone.

Before he could even tonally punctuate his question, Clotilde responded with an exuberant, "Yes! Yes, that would be great."

As they fumbled around their goodbyes, they stepped further apart and eventually made their way to their respective apartments.

CHAPTER TWELVE

On a long, narrow pad of paper stuck to the fridge with a magnet, Edward began to outline all the chores he needed to accomplish for the weekend. Grocery shopping was high on the list because he also needed to prepare lunches and meals and buy laundry detergent to clean clothes for the week ahead. Shopping was a pivotal chore, upon which many other chores depended. His list bore a strong resemblance to a flowchart.

However, despite the necessity of heading out once again, he felt oddly dreamy and a little sick to his stomach. Neither sensation was he too familiar with nor did he much care for.

Sparky nuzzled Edward's ankle. "Cat food," Edward added to the grocery list. "Sparky, you have it so easy," he mumbled. Of course, Sparky had it easy; he had a well-trained human to hunt for him, who maintained his indoor toilet facilities, and who dispensed the allotted dose of affection when he required it. Being a neutered cat, he was also not motivated by his urge to reproduce. This was yet another trait that made Sparky far superior to Edward (in Sparky's opinion) especially viewing his human in his current state of distracted open-mouthedness.

Just as Edward was about to bend down to pick up Sparky, his pocket began vibrating, causing him to startle and subsequently neglect Sparky, who was not impressed with both the interruption in the attention he was about to receive and how easily Edward was startled.

A notable sound of irritation emanated from Sparky as he scampered off in the hopes that perhaps later, Edward would muster more of his good sense and focus consistently, and effectively on the task at hand.

Edward stared at his phone. It was Daniel.

"Hey." Edward sounded remarkably calm.

"Dude! What is happening? I need updates, man! Did you find out anything? Are you still with the girl?"

Edward took the opportunity to open the fridge while Daniel asked his questions, and then wrote down, 'mayo' on his list.

"Uh... just got back and making a grocery list, which question should I answer first... hmm. OK, so no, I'm back home and not with her."

"OK, and the Rohypnol?"

"Well, it seems I *did* still have some in my system— they called it by another name, but basically, it's the same stuff."

"Shit! That's insane!"

"Yup."

"So what do you do now?"

"Uh... well, I don't know exactly. They gave me a paper in case I want to file a report."

"With the cops?"

"Yeah."

"So, who do you think did it?"

"I think it was that douchey guy who beat me up. He probably spiked the wrong drink, trying to get one of those girls sitting beside me."

"Holy shit! Dude, you need to go to the cops. Want me to come?"

"Yeah, maybe, but not today. First, I have groceries to get and laundry to do, and then Clotilde said maybe we'll do something, I don't know..." he faded off as he wrote down 'Clotilde' on his grocery list.

"One date, a trip to the blood clinic, and now you guys are inseparable?"

"No, no, it's not like that. I just kind of feel like…" Actually, Edward didn't know what he felt like, other than queasy.

"What? You met a girl, and now you lost your mind and want to get as much as you can right out of the gate. I get it. It's what I'd do."

"Daniel, that's not what it is. I actually don't feel so great."

Shift from Daniel to Jewish grandma, "Why, what's wrong?"

"I don't know. My stomach feels kind of sickish and—"

"Ohhhh! I thought you meant 'wrong' between the two of you guys!" Daniel laughed it off.

Slightly offended, Edward defended himself, "Seriously. I feel gross in my stomach."

"Do you have a fever?"

"I don't think so."

"Vomiting? Diarrhea?"

"That's a bit personal, but no."

"Uh-huh."

"Uh-huh, what?"

"You know it's actually true what they say."

"What is? You think it's the Rohypnol?" Edward was utterly confused.

"No…." Daniel's grin could be heard through the phone as Edward did laps in his tiny kitchen. "Love."

There was a lengthy pause.

"What?" Edward genuinely thought he misheard what Daniel just said.

"When you're in love, you can feel sick."

Outraged, Edward exclaimed almost normally, "C'mon! No way. That's not it. That's ridiculous. That can't even be a thing, because, like, who would— who would even want to be… and pfft, I'm not, *'in love'* or whatever. Sheesh."

"Are you finished?" Daniel interrupted Edward's rambling protest.

"Oh you know, maybe I *do* have something because I have to go to the toilet! I'll call you later after I do my stuff. Not *that* stuff, but laundry and whatnot."

"All right… you do that." Daniel was amused at how flustered Edward was. It surprised and delighted him.

"Why are you smiling?"

"Who says I'm smiling?"

"I can hear you smiling!"

"I'm not allowed to smile? Even though I'm not."

"Daniel, you're so childish. Anyway, I really gotta go."

They quickly said their good-byes. Daniel was tremendously pleased with how unraveled Edward sounded and Edward was awfully annoyed about it.

Edward was decidedly *not* in love, or whatever it was that Daniel was implying. He ran to the washroom, but he didn't have any real physical symptoms of feeling sick, other than the sick feeling itself.

He decided to sit there and wait it out while Sparky suddenly started meowing, attracted by the closed door. Edward took to the internet for answers.

He typed into the search engine, "Could love," he cringed and continued, "make you feel sick to your stomach?"

The answer appeared immediately with a whopping 110567 results, much to Edward's horror!

The first highlighted response was, "Experts agree that being newly in love gives one a queasy stomach, commonly referred to as 'butterflies in the stomach,' which is the same nervous feeling one would have before performing on stage. Love triggers your brain to release dopamine or norepinephrine hormones, which in turn divert blood away from the gut, giving that sick-to-the-stomach-feeling".

That news was more devastating than if Edward discovered he had contracted the flu! He very secretly yearned for love, even being *in* love and everything that came along with it. However, the conscious thought that he was in the midst of losing his lunch over a woman, now that he potentially had one in his grasp, was downright humiliating.

Sparky meowed louder behind the door as if in full agreement with Edward's thoughts. "You said it, Sparky! I'll be out in a second. Who needs this?" The thought repulsed Edward that his body would suffer at the mere shift in his feelings, of all things!

He tidied up the washroom quickly in an act of forcing through those wretched *feelings* and pushed aside all the queasy nonsense. He noticed the tube of toothpaste was near the end and thought, 'toothpaste' needed to be added to the list. Having marched back to the kitchen, he wrote it on the list, ripped the top sheet off the pad, shoved it in his pocket, grabbed several canvas shopping bags from the pile, and with a most determined stride headed for the door.

Waiting for the elevator, Edward felt that he had quickly overcome this foolish love business and was thankful.

CHAPTER THIRTEEN

The ride down in the elevator was obscured by Edward's not-wanting-to-think-about-anything so hard that he hadn't noticed anything at all. The doors opened downstairs when he suddenly realized there was another gentleman in the elevator car with him.

The gentleman nodded at Edward's bewildered face and exited ahead of him. Edward promptly followed behind, brushing it off, muttering to himself, "Just stop it; snap out of it." The gentleman turned around to look at Edward again, who smiled pathetically. His attempt to shuffle his feelings about only made him completely distracted to everything going on around him and then the queasiness came back. He adamantly marched to the grocery store.

"Damn it!" he thought. "I'm a grown man!" He wrestled with the locking mechanism on the shopping cart. A young boy who was sitting on the bench waiting for his mother, dryly called out, "You only put in a quarter."

"What?" Edward replied, snapping into reality again.

"It takes a dollar. You only put in twenty-five cents."

A second-snap back to reality, Edward calmed down and replied, "Oh... I see. Thank you." Fumbling through the contents of his pocket for the correct coin, a few people had gathered behind him waiting to acquire a cart.

As he energetically pulled his hand from his pocket, believing he had at least one coin of every denomination, Edward managed to dislodge most of the coins like confetti from a rocket onto the floor. They went pinging and clanking under the carts, and one even rolled on its edge far past the boy on the bench until it spun into a spiral and collapsed about six meters away.

This was just fantastic. The lady and older man who were trying to get carts for themselves suddenly stopped to assist Edward in retrieving his coins, and the little boy chased after the run-away nickel. Edward felt a wave of embarrassment wash over him, which not only eclipsed his queasiness; it made him downright distressed!

"Thank you, thank you, don't worry about it." Edwards tried to get over with collecting his coins. He didn't care about any that he might have lost; he just wanted his cart so he could get through the store anonymously like usual and go home.

Edward stepped back and looked through the collection of coins in his hand. He let the other people get their carts ahead of him as he pulled the dollar coin from his palm. Inadvertently he let out a hefty sigh and proceeded to get his cart. As fate would have it, his attempt to not draw attention to himself failed as Edward pushed around his squeaky cart. The rear left wheel made a shrill donkey-like squeal followed by a grating sound whenever he tried turning.

It was a highly rhythmic tune, if perhaps only for a colony of insects at a cook-out, sitting 'round the bonfire, singing songs. For human ears, it was likely on the list of banned torture methods from Guantanamo Bay, ranking slightly worse than waterboarding.

Eventually, Edward managed to get everything on his list and successfully proceeded through the self-checkout lane. He had never used it before, but he was desperate to avoid any further human interaction at this establishment.

Edward was mentally exhausted and simply zoned out until he was back home, separating his laundry. It wasn't even intentional; he just couldn't think anymore. No more "what-ifs" or "isn't love stupid" thoughts. Right now, it was all about creating piles of navy blue and black, mediums, and the beige-whites-light blues on the floor of his bedroom.

Sparky sprawled out at the foot of Edward's bed, letting out a stretchy 'meowwww,' which caught Edward's attention finally.

Sparky, of course, didn't care and rolled right over, turning his back to Edward. He was displeased with Edward's inattentiveness.

A buzzing was coming from down the hall as Edward brought the first load of laundry to the stacked machines in the closet. He filled the detergent receptacle. He triple-checked that the front-facing door was locked and made certain that the water temperatures were set for cold-wash and cold-rinse. He almost forgot to press "start" and shook his head. It was really beginning to get to him— all this "lack of access to brain function" business.

With an exasperated flutter of his eyelids, Edward shlepped to the kitchen. He proceeded to pull out his bucket of household cleaning products, a system his mother had created for him that served him rather well ever since he left home.

He stood there and stared at it blankly until he realized the buzzing was persisting. Edward searched for his phone. Somehow it had managed to hide itself under a dishcloth on the counter when Edward returned home.

Six text messages, two missed calls and a voicemail.

Daniel.

Without even bothering to read anything or listen to the message, Edward just turned his ringer back on, dialled Daniel and went hands-free so he could keep on with what he was doing.

"Dude, I'm downstairs!" answered Daniel. 'Dude' was usually his standard greeting, often followed by a statement or a question. He rarely ever said, 'hi' or 'hello' when it came to Edward.

"Downstairs where?" mumbled Edward as he moved things around on the counter.

"I was just about to ring your doorbell!" exclaimed Daniel.

As stunned as Edward was by Daniel's sudden intrusion, it might be precisely what he needed to break out of this funk he found himself in. Edward buzzed Daniel in, unlocked the door and left it just slightly ajar, and resumed his chores in the kitchen.

Snappy, quick-shuffled steps approached the door, and Edward was ready for him. Daniel bounded in, moderately out of breath and swiftly turned around to lock the door, obviously a habitual action.

"My mom made you some food!" Daniel plopped a red, rectangular Tupperware container down on the counter exactly where Edward had just cleaned. Edward glared at Daniel, but he was oblivious.

"Wait - what? Why did your mom make me food? It's early afternoon."

"Well, I told her you were all meshuggeneh over this chick and—"

Edward stopped moving, his body stood firmly in place, and his eyes glared even more pointedly at Daniel. "You told your mom I was crazy over a *girl*?!" he exclaimed in a deep, infuriated whisper. How was this helping Edward's condition?

"Open it." Daniel gestured to Edward, completely ignoring any speck of indignation emanating from him. "Your Yiddish is getting better, by the way, and yes, yes, I did tell her because she loves you like a son and is always asking about you. So fucking shoot me. Open it."

Edward began to open the container while still staring at Daniel. It was hard to stay mad at him.

"Oh, smoked meat sandwiches!" Edward suddenly sounded uncharacteristically sweet and delicate.

"Uh-huh. You're welcome."

"Mmm mustard," Edward mumbled with delight as he took a bite. He leaned up against the fridge. "Aren't you having one?"

"No, I ate already."

"Oh my god, these are so good." Mumbled Edward as he stuffed in as much of half a sandwich as he could. "Crazy. Your mom sho-[mumble] restaurant." Edward's eyes were closing and rolling with pleasure while he let out muffled sighs of deep satisfaction. Daniel confidently grinned with his arms folded across his chest.

Daniel loved seeing Edward so messed up. It wasn't a bad thing; if Edward were downtrodden, Daniel wouldn't be happy at all. This was different. Edward was utterly loopy, and it was wonderful.

"Tell your mom thanks from me. These are amazing." Edward came up for air.

"Of course."

"How does food solve this problem? It just does." Rhetorically Edward asked and answered the question.

Daniel was pleased. "Ok, so what's next?"

"What d'you mean?"

"Like today, with you, her, tomorrow, stuff... ya know... etcetera?"

"Etcetera? Well, I uh... I don't know. I'm just going forward... with 'stuff'"

Daniel stared at Edward's head as he gobbled down the rest of the first sandwich. The laser-hot beams of Daniel's glare were obviously felt by Edward, who suddenly stopped and looked up.

"What?!" Edward asked in a more natural, irritated way. Daniel just stared intently.

"Oh! Oh? That! Uh... well I hadn't planned... you know, I don't know when— or *if*, that's going to happen..." he stuffed more sandwich in his face, if for no other reason than to just stop blathering on.

"Uh-huh," Daniel wasn't impressed. Nor was he fooled. "So, you *haven't* thought about it?" He paused at length for dramatic effect. "Did you buy new condoms?"

Edward's eyes shot up and locked in on Daniel. "*New* condoms? No, Daniel, they have recycled, secondhand ones now!" The choice of Daniel's words helped deflect the question.

Daniel thought about it for a second, and they both started laughing with repulsion.

Edward jokingly admitted, "Yeah, yeah, so I stocked up, all right? You happy?" He tried not to grin, but it was impossible.

Daniel smacked Edward on the side of the arm as Edward was about to take a bite making him slightly miss the sandwich. "Atta boy! Good, good."

Edward looked up as mustard had rubbed across his cheek outside his mouth from Daniel's enthusiastic arm-whacking - which might have been an intentional jab back for Edward's mocking him on the 'new' condoms remark. Daniel was good at those.

"And what about the drug thing? Are you going to go to the cops or what?" Daniel pressed.

"I told you. Yeah, I probably will. I just don't know exactly when."

"And when's your next date with Clotilde?"

"I don't know. Maybe today."

"Ah, right. House cleaning. Fresh laundry. I get it."

"Daniel, I do that anyway on weekends."

"Sure you do, buddy." and he slapped Edward's other arm just as the last piece of the second sandwich was about to pop into Edward's mouth. Now Edward knew for sure that Daniel was doing it on purpose. Sadly, that was just enough of a jolt that Edward dropped the piece onto the floor.

Daniel didn't mean to do that. They both stared at it while Daniel gasped. "Shit!"

"What the hell?"

"Dude, I'm sorry." and he started to laugh. Edward did too.

"I'm telling your mother! You little fucker!"

"Yeah, use that language in front of my mother, and you'll never see another sandwich again! She thinks you're 'such a sweet boy,'" Daniel mimicked his mother with a shrill and feeble voice.

Edward responded with a speedy, albeit immature, flick to Daniel's ear. Daniel let out an overdramatic yelp while simultaneously laughing at Edward's cat-like reflexes.

CHAPTER FOURTEEN

The metal zippers and buttons whirring and clanking around the dryer finally came to a halt. The last of Edward's laundry was done, and the apartment was the cleanest and most organized it had been in a long time.

The speed at which Edward scurried back and forth throughout the place also kept his mind preoccupied with something other than Clotilde. Even Daniel's visit helped lighten the intensity of Edward's emotions.

Edward stood majestically in the hallway with his feet anchored, observing his accomplishments. The bedroom was no longer scruffy looking, the bathroom was glistening, the kitchen counter was visible and uncluttered, and the living room was neat and orderly. Perhaps Edward's place had never looked this well-maintained. Clotilde had seen it before, but Edward was sure it hadn't been for long enough to form a permanent depiction in her mind but rather a temporary and fleeting impression only.

He swaggered to the living room and sat down on the sofa. Sparky hopped up beside him, but Edward quickly shoed him off, much to the feline's dismay. This had never happened before!

"Sparky, I just cleaned everything! We don't need your cat fur covering everything just yet." Edward explained aloud. Sparky was not at all impressed by a single word of it, but amazed that Edward could even speak when he obviously had taken leave from the vast majority of his faculties!

A guilty feeling overtook Edward straight away, as he also realized that he never had not allowed Sparky on the sofa. He decided to swing his legs up and lie down the length of the sofa, tapping his stomach to beckon Sparky back up. It was preferable to sit on Edward rather than the sofa, and Sparky was instantly reassured by the gesture. He hopped up, tucked his limbs beneath him, stared into Edward's face giving him a drowsy slow pair of blinks. For just a moment, Edward was very comfortable and somewhat self-congratulatory. He decided to close his eyes and think about how marvellous he was for having done such a phenomenal job cleaning his apartment.

Then he fell asleep. He slept deeply. He slept for three hours and twelve minutes undisturbed.

Eventually, even Edward's own subconscious mind was desperately trying to introduce fire alarms and rushing waves, and other noisy imagery to him so that he would wake up. None of that worked. It was time to bring out the big guns: Clotilde.

Edward dreamed he was paddling along in a canoe, blissfully unaware. The sun shone down, making the lake's surface twinkle and shine. He slowly turned behind him, with an idiotic grin upon his face, to gaze upon Clotilde. She was sitting towards the rear of the canoe, smiling at Edward sympathetically with a tinge of pity.

Edward bolted upright on the sofa in one quick swoop as he felt the canoe topple over. "Clotilde!" he gasped. Sparky sprung away and hid. Heavily panicked, Edward realized he was not paddling along a calm, sparkling lake, but instead sleeping his opportunities away at home. The room was dark, and he galloped about much like a lanky foal if he were also able to turn lamps on and mutter, "Shit, shit, shit!" at every turn.

Having tracked down his phone, Edward noticed the ringer was off, and there had been two text messages, one missed call and a voicemail. He keyed in his password twice due to nervous fumbling.

The texts were from Clotilde. The call was also Clotilde and obviously, the voicemail would be from her as well. Edward felt like Sparky tricked him, suddenly misaligned with fate or was cursed, to fall asleep the way he did. Wasn't there some Greek myth about such a thing? If there wasn't, there certainly should be, Edward thought. "The brave and triumphant Edwardius lulled to sleep by the demi-god Sparkius, only to awaken fifty years later to a completely different world where the maiden of his dreams is an old cursed hag."

"Snap out of it!" Edward yelled to himself. Not only was Edward shaky and out of sorts after waking up so abruptly, but he was fuming over the fact he missed three whole hours of his day.

The first text from Clotilde read, "Hey. Wondering if you gave any thought to doing something this evening?" It was neutral, emotionally benign, but Edward knew better than to feel relieved just yet.

The second message read, "You're probably doing all those chores you were talking about. I'll try calling you." Edward was cringing. He was never that guy who could fake being aloof because apparently, people do that. Especially pertaining to Clotilde, 'aloof' was the last thing he wanted to appear like, second only to appearing too eager.

Hesitantly, Edward moved on to the voicemail. "Hi, Edward. It's Clotilde." She sighed in that whispery buttery way that she did. "Umm... I realize this is the third text or message I'm leaving and they all probably going to the same phone and if you can't hear or respond to the first one, you probably won't be able to answer the call. Um so... yeah, I was hoping to meet up, but if you can't or don't want to, that's ok too. Bye."

Edward was both too self-absorbed and not astute enough to realize that Clotilde was feeling increasingly disappointed with traces of insecurity. All Edward thought was that he was stupid for having fallen asleep so unexpectedly. He immediately called her.

As if Clotilde was almost not going to answer the call, she picked up at the last moment.

"Hello?" She said calmly but pleasantly, not expecting the conversation to amount to much.

"Hi!" Exclaimed Edward rather over exuberantly and breathlessly. He just couldn't win. It was difficult for him to gauge the output of his emotional responses and they were often askew.

Clotilde perked up a little. "Hi! I wasn't expecting to hear from you."

"Really? Why?"

Clotilde was about to elaborate, but Edward interrupted her to explain himself first.

"You know what happened?"

"No, what happened?"

"Well, I'm an idiot."

"Why are you an idiot?"

"I don't know *why*... I just *happen* to be. I might be borderline narcoleptic..."

"What?" Clotilde was confused and thought Edward was trying to convey some bad news about himself.

"I mean, I fell asleep on the couch!" He ashamedly blurted out.

Clotilde started to laugh with relief. "Oh!! Well, you were tired. Did you do all your chores, at least?"

"Yes, yes, I did, and Daniel brought me his mom's smoke meat and I guess I just crashed when everything was finished. I didn't hear the phone and I woke up all stupid and it was dark and..."

Balance was restored. Clotilde seemed perfectly normal and Edward was babbling.

"Oh, that's fine. I just thought maybe you had other plans or were busy or..."

"Plans? No, I don't usually have other plans... I mean Daniel, sometimes and myself, but not tonight I don't have any and I saw him already with the meat like I said." Edward hated the fact that he constantly felt like he was crashing and burning.

Clotilde was amused; she actually loved the way Edward fumbled and rambled and secretly wished he would never lose that. "So, what's the deal with the smoke meat?" She asked, thinking she was helping Edward move forward over the hurdles of the conversation.

"The smoke meat? Uh..." Edward couldn't tell her the real reason why Daniel's mother sent it over. "Well, she uh, she had made too much, and uh... didn't want it to go to waste."

"Too much? I didn't realize that was even a thing!" It didn't sound like Clotilde was buying it.

"I mean, yeah, it was a lot."

"Oh... so you probably don't feel like eating dinner."

"Oh no, I do, I do. Totally. I mean, yeah, I ate them both. Both sandwiches - but I would go eat with you... are you even asking me that? Shit." Never mind the earlier crashing and burning, Edward was now dive-bombing full-flame straight into a barrel of gun powder.

Listening to Edward unravel made Clotilde much more at ease. Although Edward, in his befuddlement, could not see that Clotilde wasn't as surefooted as she appeared.

Clotilde decided to take some initiative as well as cut the tension for Edward. "Well, if you want to come over, we could always order in."

Edward paused; he wasn't expecting Clotilde to suggest that. Her statement relieved some of Edward's tension. However, he started to feel the butterflies in his stomach begin to awaken and spread up to his chest, not to mention radiate outward to other regions of his body.

"Edward? Are you there?" She nudged.

"Yes, yes, of course! I was just thinking— maybe I answered you in my head. Gotta remember to do that out loud!" He laughed awkwardly and Clotilde followed suit.

"You're very funny."

"Am I? Oh, good. I'm glad you think so," Edward admitted. Sometimes in his bungling way, he managed to appear as if his awkwardness was somewhat intentional and perhaps even intelligently designed. It certainly flowed that way with Daniel, but rarely with anyone else.

All the cleaning, arranging, washing, and organizing was almost for nothing, Edward thought. He didn't want to let on that it was such an involved set of tasks because Clotilde would believe that he neglects his housework— which he does to some degree. He also didn't want her to know that the chores exhausted him to the point of passing out for several hours in the early evening.

Instead, Edward readily conceded to an evening at Clotilde's house, almost as if he was indifferent about the whole affair. This, of course, was another of his defense mechanisms kicking in, which attempted to keep him from getting too excited or ahead of himself. The butterflies were still there but were kept at bay for the time being.

They set a date for just slightly later than the time it would take Edward to pick up a bottle of wine and travel to Clotilde's. Edward was ready; he was ready hours ago, but regardless, he spent the last few minutes fussing around the house, fussing with his hair, and leaving some extra food and a full bowl of water for Sparky.

Edward could feel Sparky's unimpressed stare. "What?" Edward asked aloud. "Don't look at me like that. You get extra food and water just in case I'm late." Speaking of which, Edward went to search for that fresh box of condoms that he bought. He opened the nightstand drawer and took a good look at the unopened box. "Variety Pack?" He read on the front as if for the first time.

In fact, it was the first time. Edward hadn't bought the package that he thought he did. Edward began reading the types of condoms contained within the 'Variety Pack.' Much to his dismay, some of them sounded outlandishly exotic if not downright pretentious!

Initially, the only questions he had about the matter were, "How many to bring along? How many is too many? Or should I even bring any tonight— is it too presumptuous?"

But now, the questions, and more importantly, their answers became critical. Edward grappled with the idea that perhaps he wouldn't be able to match the level of expertise that fancy condoms commanded and that by selecting any of these, Clotilde would have unreasonably high expectations. Edward was, at the very most, a very regular guy who used very ordinary condoms and who, by his own analysis, probably resembled a malnour-ished, albino, gazelle caught in a trap when endeavouring to have sex. He was a realist in this way, however a tad harsh towards himself.

Swirling his index finger around the array of mockingly colourful packets splayed out on the bed, Edward closed his eyes and picked two. He refused to read what he had selected and shoved them into his non-wallet back pocket.

Sparky sprung up onto the pillow. The sound of the packets being picked up and put back in the box enticed him. "You only live once, eh Sparky!" uncharacteristically announced Edward. Sparky squinted at him as if to express deep dissatisfaction. Despite Edward being a stupid human, Sparky truly did love him.

CHAPTER FIFTEEN

With a bagged bottle of cabernet franc clenched securely under his arm, Edward approached Clotilde's apartment building. Peering into the glare of his phone, he verified that the address was correct and searched for the buzzer code. It might have only been due to the cool evening air, but Edward was remarkably calm. The flustered Edward that rambled on earlier in the evening was temporarily suppressed, not unlike a frozen frog that can withstand subzero winter temperatures only to be thawed and returned to its typical hopping self when the weather warms up.

Edward typed 2-2-2-2# into the keypad and waited. The moment Clotilde answered, all of Edward's butterflies returned, but his emotions shifted toward anticipation more than the plain queasiness he had not yet grown accustomed to. Usually, he was more comfortable responding to initiated actions of others. He could take action once the wheels were in motion but often did not set the wheels in motion to anything himself, except for those few things solely pertaining to his personal maintenance and responsibility.

"Come in. It's unit 108 on the left." She said without Edward saying a word. Just as he opened his mouth to confirm, the buzzer loudly drowned him out, and he jumped to grab the door handle before the buzzing stopped. He almost dropped the wine bottle, which did little for his butterflies.

Edward skipped into the lobby and realized he was breathing rather heavily. He had only seconds to calm down, which would prove to be unlikely at all because, as he turned the corner to proceed down the hall, Clotilde had stepped out from her apartment smiling and waving. Thankfully, Edward was now holding the paper bag very tightly around the neck of the wine bottle as his shoe snagged the carpet, and he almost tripped again. He tried to ignore it completely, but Clotilde snickered.

"What's so funny?" Asked Edward, as he decided he should probably just be himself.

"Oh nothing; I always laugh when people almost trip. You looked very serious until that last second." Clotilde gestured for Edward to enter her place.

"Well, I was *very* serious. I almost dropped the wine outside, too." he figured he might as well confess to all of it, seeing as Clotilde appeared to find Edward's clumsiness endearing.

The colours of Clotilde's apartment were as warm and comforting as everything else about her. Edward felt like he had stepped into a cozy cottage rather than an urban condo.

"Wow, this is really nice." He stood still taking it all in.

"Thanks. Take off your clothes and let me take the wine from you... unless you're still afraid to let it go."

"Did you just say, 'take off your clothes'?" Edward started to giggle as he handed her the bottle.

Embarrassed, Clotilde started to laugh too. "I meant coat! A coat is a piece of clothing, too, you know." Edward was just happy that the dynamics were shifting.

"Well, I don't know about that." Edward mused. "You know, that's how it starts, and then the next thing is you're putting Rohypnol in my drink! Which is why *I'm* in charge of supplying the beverages, for the time being, thank you very much. If you could keep that where I can see it, please, I just can't trust anyone these days!"

Completely smitten and smiling, Clotilde stared at him intensely, although Edward couldn't read what she was emoting whatsoever; he was just being playfully at ease. He took his coat off and threw it over the back of her dining chair as if to punctuate his statement.

Clotilde rushed forward and stood within a couple of centimetres of him, much to Edward's surprise. "You think I *need* to use Rohypnol on you?" She smiled seductively looking at all the parts of Edward's face. *This,* he could sense. The balance had shifted again, and he felt the temperature in the room suddenly go from autumn to midsummer.

Steadily, Edward looked down at her and with all the self-control he could muster said, "Yes..."

"Yes, I need to sedate you in order to have my way with you?"

"Have your way with me? Is that why you lured me here to this, this *place*? Give me back that bottle!" Clotilde was giggling as Edward jokingly reached for the wine. Clotilde blocked him.

"Really? Do you realize how long my arms are?"

Clotilde stood between Edward and the wine. "I don't care how long your arms are."

Edward reached around her with both arms, bending down slightly to reach for the bottle with his right hand while his left hand held her lower back to keep her close and not have her tip backward. "Who was this guy?" Edward thought to himself. "Where did these moves come from?"

He pretended to be unable to reach the bottle so Clotilde pushed forward against him with the entire front of her body. That caught Edward's attention; feelings began to arise.

"Ummm, excuse me, Miss? Miss, you are invading my personal space over here."

"*Your* personal space? This is *my* personal space!"

"Over here, right here is my— personal— space!" He said. They paused and stared at each other. Then Clotilde just went for it, stood on her toes and planted her lips forcefully on his. Edward didn't resist and even melted a little.

"How's *that* for invading your personal sp-" She was cut off because Edward forcefully and uncharacteristically kissed her right back. That was all it took for the two of them to go at it in the dining room like a couple of sex-starved lab rats. Clothes were flung, furniture was getting knocked over, condom wrappers were opening and nobody cared to read what type they were.

Impressively, Edward was pulling out techniques he didn't know he had and Clotilde was exuberantly appreciative. He managed to do his naked albino gazelle dance throughout every room of Clotilde's condo which was more action than it had ever seen. Not surprisingly, it was more action than Edward ever had to dole out. Not that he *had to* do anything, but it was somehow naturally effortless and monumental simultaneously.

After an evening of rampant cavorting, they worked up quite the appetites and ordered food, opened the wine, sat down cozily upon the couch looking like they had just done a half-marathon (uphill, both ways, in a jungle).

"Now that we got that out of the way!" Clotilde exclaimed as she stuffed a forkful of food in her mouth.

"Out of the way?" Edward felt very at ease and was hamming it up. "I feel so used." He stuffed a larger amount of food in his mouth.

"But did you like it?" Clotilde asked sweetly.

Edward paused, and although he tried to keep his face emotionless by sucking in his cheeks, he couldn't help a little smirk creep up. "Yes, I sure did."

Not only had Edward's inhibitions all but completely dissolved, he felt strangely normal. It wasn't 'normal' in the way he 'normally felt', but he felt like he was finally a normal person and not fluttering on the edge of what he wished he was doing, never expecting actually to be participating in it.

He had been in a few relationships with females of various sorts before but never where he felt so tranquil while simultaneously being this aroused and with this much confidence, especially when Clotilde was someone who typically embodied traits that would intimidate him. All the while, he felt a fluidity of self-assuredness that he never had with anyone but Daniel - and that was certainly not in a sexual way. It seemed that not only was Clotilde entirely on board with it all Edward had going for himself, but she was also— dare he thought— equally, passionately captivated by him.

This was truly a pleasant departure from the old Edward, who never would have gone to a costume party alone. The further he propelled himself forward, the more he realized how pivotal that night was for him. Fate could have unveiled itself in numerous ways, but he was beginning to sense the merit in it emerging this way. Yes, it started off a little painfully, but he looked at where he was just a few days later, and he was extremely grateful that he pushed past the discomfort and humiliation.

In one of his electives back when he was at university, Edward had learned that evolution in nature is often neither slow nor gradual. Species generally don't gradually mutate; they go through long periods of stasis, then something changes in their environment, and in order to survive, they needed to suddenly adapt and consequently evolve. He had understood it in theory but now he felt like he was experiencing it in a real way— maybe not on a cellular level, but profoundly and irreversibly, nonetheless.

Edward wondered what the final result would be, a week or month from now. What would *that* Edward look like? Was this an uncovering of the authentic Edward or a morphing from the old one to an entirely new one? There was a distinct difference, he contemplated. As comfortable as he was about the whole arrangement, especially how things had progressed with Clotilde, he was still primarily apprehensive about the litany of unknown qualities that the new (or recently unveiled) Edward might possess.

Once again, a sharp poke to Edward's ribs from Clotilde suddenly returned him to the present moment. The pondering could be resumed later. For now, it was time to pay attention to the conversation at hand.

"I have a twelve-hour shift tomorrow," whispered Clotilde reluctantly. Edward was often slow, but not stupid and realized this was his cue.

"Yeah, I should go. We have a new department head starting tomorrow and my co-worker, Judy wants us to form some sort of 'sub-department.'"

"What kind of sub-department?" asked Clotilde, genuinely interested.

"I really have no idea. To be honest, she really freaks me out, and so I just go along with stuff even though I have no idea what she's talking about, until it actually comes to pass." Admitted Edward.

"That doesn't sound like you at all!" laughed Clotilde.

"Are you being serious or sarcastic?" Edward truly wasn't sure.

"I'm serious." Clotilde was still laughing, so Edward became even more confused.

"You're laughing!"

"You always seem so self-assured."

"Are you kidding me?" Edward was stunned, bewildered, and mildly amused. "I don't believe anyone has ever accused me of that before." He proceeded to collect his things and put on his coat. He scanned the condo and noticed it had become significantly tousled since his arrival.

"Sorry about the mess; I'm not sure how that happened." Although he knew perfectly well how it happened, he was still surprised. Thoughts of what his Monday was going to look like began to creep into his consciousness.

Edward and Clotilde exchanged another uncharacteristically passionate goodbye and then parted ways at the lobby door. The exterior glass door had started to frost up, and Edward felt he should hurry home before it got too cold.

Clotilde had turned to walk back to her suite when Edward decided to call for a cab. All this tenderhearted warmth he was carrying about himself being penetrated by the inhospitable icy night air, was not a sensation he was looking forward to. It wasn't that far a ride home anyway, and he reassured himself that he could easily afford this rare indulgence.

Within moments the taxi arrived, and Edward bounded down the front steps, opened the car door, and folded his gangly limbs into the backseat.

"You're a very tall fellow, aren't ya?" commented the driver.

As if Edward had never heard that before, "Yes, could you take me to 444 Clairvale Court, please," and turned his head to gaze out the window while he impatiently rubbed his hands together. The cabbie was smart enough to clue in that Edward didn't feel like chatting about his height or anything else.

Periodically, the driver would look back through the rearview mirror and notice Edward's rosy cheeks. He didn't know that it wasn't the cold that had them so flushed, but rather Edward's energetic escapades that night, which he was still reminiscing about.

As the cab pulled up to the curb, Edward had a ten-dollar bill ready to pay for the eight-dollar fare. The two-dollar tip was thanks for not chattering all the way home.

"Thanks, man," Edward mumbled as he unfolded himself onto the sidewalk and ran towards his building. In the lobby, he was met with a giddy man and two equally giggly women draped over each arm. "This must be that guy!" Edward thought. He and the trio exchanged a few awkward, but silly glances as they waited for the elevator.

Once inside, Edward stood to the front left corner opposite the button panel and saw that they had pressed the floor above his. Now he was sure it was the group he heard through the bathroom pipes. They didn't look like what he imagined at all, and he found himself turning to stare at them more often than was necessary, or even polite, for such a short ride.

Having become somewhat self-conscious, Edward exited without a glance back and rushed to his door. Sparky was patiently awaiting his return, until that moment when he unleashed a series of plaintive meows.

"Oh, I'm sorry, Sparky. Did you miss me?" Edward sympathized with his cat's complaints while he hung up his coat and took off his shoes. Sparky proceeded to nuzzle Edward's feet and ankles, purring loudly. Edward squatted down and picked Sparky up and walked to the bedroom, where he began to tell his feline companion about the evening's escapades.

"Sparky, my boy; you have no idea what your old master was up to this evening!" He went on as he disrobed and climbed into bed. "I can't even begin to tell you!" Sparky nestled in a neatly wrapped circle on the crumpled covers beside Edward in the spot designated for him. Sparky didn't care about Edward's evening, or why he smelled like Clotilde but was just pleased to have him back on schedule.

Edward adjusted the alarm to give himself an extra ten minutes to be sure he had his lunch prepared but also, just in case he was dragging his feet come morning. Within barely three seconds of turning over, Edward fell asleep.

CHAPTER SIXTEEN

Monday morning slammed into Edward's consciousness in what felt like seven whole minutes after he shut his eyes. Even Sparky was thrown off his game by the incessant, jagged beeps of his alarm clock. Today, in particular, was not a day to wake up in such an unsettled manner.

Initially, Edward thought he hadn't set the time correctly. It was still relatively dark in his room and he felt simply awful. How could such a delightful evening, full of sexual shenanigans, leave him feeling utterly depleted, he wondered. Clearly, Edward had not experienced this enough to know that what he was experiencing was not only completely normal but expected.

He began to rush around aimlessly before muttering to himself and focusing on a single direction. "Shower, shower, yeah, first shower." As he shuffled around like a wounded moth making his way to the washroom. Sparky, as was so often the case, wasn't impressed and did his morning stretches where he lay.

"I'll get to you in a minute!" called Edward from the bathroom. Sparky proceeded to the kitchen on his own to scoop out any leftover kibble from his dish. The shower started up and Sparky could hear clanking, banging, and swearing. As long as there was still food to eat, he refused to be concerned about it. The array of shampoo and plastic body wash bottles had fallen, and Edward was clumsily trying to keep everything in order, although he still felt unsettled and slightly dehydrated.

The water was turned off, and Edward comforted himself with a thick fuzzy towel in which he buried his face. After a few moments, he let out a deep, bellowing sigh, shook his head and started to dry off the rest of himself. He stooped to look at his reflection in the foggy mirror. "At least you don't look as bad you feel, mister!" which gave him a little relief that he could actually pull off the "this is just any old Monday, Edward" routine at work.

Edward's goopy, discoloured eye was now practically nonexistent. Things felt manageable again, and his head began to clear up. He selected an outfit slightly spiffier than usual without being dressy. It was, after all, the first day with the new department head and although he couldn't care less, he knew Judy cared a great deal.

He's had worse Mondays. Despite feeling hungover, Edward was still reeling with the blissful disbelief of what transpired last night between him and Clotilde. He dared not dwell too long upon it, as he knew it could begin to unravel him and today was not a good day to be unraveled by something that should, by no stretch of the imagination, have any negative connotation!

But Edward was good at stretching his imagination, and although he hadn't done so in a long time, there was a heightened sense of insecurity puddling around his sub-conscience ever since he met Clotilde. At this precise moment, that vulnerability should have been greatly muted, and Edward knew that. He hung on to that and repressed any urge to talk himself out of how wonderful he felt.

The truth of the matter was, Edward felt uncharacteristically elated. Were he able to let his guard down, he would realize that all the negative self-chatter in the world couldn't ruin this moment. It was real. Clotilde genuinely liked him. She saw him for who he was and still liked him; she liked him a great deal.

Edward got all his work things ready, including his lunch, put on his coat and went through all the ritualistic turning off of switches and turning on the radio for Sparky.

Slipping out the door with one glove partially on and one gripped in his teeth, Edward mumbled a good-bye to Sparky, who squeezed out a deep, "I love you" blink at him, which went entirely unnoticed. The door was locked and the keys slipped clanking into his pocket. Edward pulled the second glove on as he proceeded to the elevator.

He hadn't the faintest idea why having a new department head was making him flutter so and just racked it up to his lack of sleep. The elevator barely reached the lobby when Edward's pocket started to vibrate.

Of course, it was Daniel. Edward knew how Mondays typically unfolded. It usually started with Daniel either being anxious, excited, or exhausted and a text message was always the delivery method.

"Dude. Whatcha think the new dept head'll be like? U ready?" read the text.

The other thing Edward could count on without fail was Daniel's habitual use of the word, 'dude'. However, Edward didn't have a worthwhile answer for Daniel, but he knew that if he didn't reply, Daniel would panic, and so he simply replied, "Dunno."

Of course, Daniel wouldn't be satisfied with that response, but Edward chose to ignore any further interaction until he got to work. At least Daniel would know Edward was on his way. The weather had turned to its permanent colder autumn temperatures, and therefore there would be no checking of cell phones or ungloving for any nonemergency.

Edward was unaware that he was exhibiting signs of nervousness scuttling in to work this morning; he noticed the palpitations but assumed they were due to the cold and his quickened pace. What he failed to realize was that on some level, he knew this was a very important day.

A lady with a rolling briefcase almost tripped Edward as she crossed in front of him without looking back as he entered the lobby of his workplace. It wasn't always easy for people to estimate how much distance Edward covered with his lanky stride; he had a lengthy gait and could suddenly arrive at a destination in half the time of a regular, shorter person.

Daniel was pacing in a spastic circular fashion near the elevators until he spotted Edward march across the lobby.

"*There* you are!" Daniel mumbled as Edward approached. Edward wasn't sure what the fuss was about, "I'm not late, am I?"

"No, no, you're not late; I just wanted to go up there together in case Judy caught me right off the elevator."

"And so?" Edward was confused.

"She's going to want to talk about the sub-department group thing and I honestly have nothing." Daniel was readjusting his hair repeated, pulling it back into his elastic tie as he and Edward got on the elevator. Edward observed Daniel's frustration.

"Did your hair shrink or something? You seem to be having a hard time with that."

"Dude, it's not funny. I had a tiny, little trim and now some pieces aren't reaching. It's making me crazy." Just as he thought he managed to pull all the hair back into a ponytail with no strays, a forceful curly ringlet sprung out from the front. Daniel let out a deep sorrowful sigh and then tucked the strand behind one ear.

Edward couldn't relate to such things and looked at Daniel with bewilderment. "Anyway," he tried to bring the conversation back to the fundamental matter at hand. "What's the big deal about this new department head and the sub-department thing? I don't get it."

He was partially posing the question to Daniel, but he was also becoming aware that it did feel important to Edward, too, although he didn't know why.

The doors opened on their floor, and Daniel tried holding the unruly clump of hair to the side of his head as they exited. "I don't know, Edward; it just is!" he whispered. It was one of those answers a parent gives to their child, out of frustration when they've asked too many times or when the parent can't provide an adequate reply.

"Well, we're no further ahead," Edward muttered back.

Judy wasn't at her desk, and so the two of them slinked past and down the last row alongside the windows to their cubicles. Before too long, Daniel and Edward picked up their usual routines and started to work on existing projects, getting lost in thought and forgetting about the new department head and Judy.

Suddenly Daniel whispered to Edward as he overheard Judy's voice speaking with uncharacteristic exuberance, "She's here, she's here." Edward stood up just enough to see over the upper edge of his wall. He scanned the area and saw Judy turned to one side, arms folded, chatting with a young man whose arm and shoulder could be seen. Edward could hear a couple of grunts of confirmation from him but that was all.

Edward fell back down to his seat a millisecond before Judy turned to look at him. He leaned back in his chair to whisper back at Daniel, "That must be the guy."

Daniel slowly stood up to catch a glimpse and saw a little more of the fellow than Edward had and sat back down. "I can't see anything; nothing significant anyway."

"Should we just wait here, or do we go over?" mumbled Daniel to Edward.

"You can go over if you want. I'm not the mingling type. If she wants us over there, she'll come and get us," declared Edward. Daniel and Edward continued to whisper and chat about what to do.

"You're right. I don't want to look like a kiss-ass. Once you start down that eager-beaver road, they'll expect it all the time, then it's all downhill from there." Agreed Daniel.

Edward nodded and turned back to his desk as Judy seemed to appear beside them out of nowhere. "Guys, come and meet the new department head, Troy," and she gestured without hesitation for the pair to follow her.

Daniel mouthed the name 'Troy' to Edward with a gagging gesture. Edward concurred with a sour expression. It seemed neither of them was fond of the name.

As they approached the front of the office, Judy announced, "Troy, I'd like to introduce you to two of our finest programmers,

Daniel and Edward." And with that, the man in his crisply ironed silver-grey shirt and light tweed slacks slowly pivoted around on his tasseled loafers. He had rose-blond highlights, a fake tan, and a very pretentious grimace on his face exposing his unnaturally fluorescent white teeth. Edward peered into his eyes as he thrust his right hand forward for a shake.

"Hi, Edward," he announced to Troy, who responded with, "Pleasure, Edward," as he gave him an excessively firm handshake. It was more like a hand-*crushing* than a shake. Edward looked down as Troy's voice rang through his ears. He stared at his unyielding grip on his hand. Troy's knuckles were scraped and he was already looking at Daniel.

Edward started to quiver, his heart palpitating, and beads of sweat began to appear on his upper lip. Troy let go and grabbed Daniel's hand, "Daniel! Hi." Daniel replied, trying to emulate Troy's firmness and confidence, "Hi Troy!" but his hand wasn't as strong as Edward's and was obviously hurting. He flashed a brief, irritated look toward Edward, who was boiling from the inside out and didn't notice Daniel's subtle reaction.

Troy condescendingly looked at them both and laughed, "Programmers, eh? I guess somebody's got to do it!"

Edward was fired up and without a second thought, wrapped his left hand around Troy's throat and waved his right hand, which was in a clammy fist at Troy's face. Judy screamed! "Edward! What the heck!?" It was only the second time Judy called Edward by the correct name.

Daniel was in disbelief. "Dude! It was a joke."

Troy's face turned red as he tried to unclench Edward's fingers from his neck. "Temper, temper! Are you fucking crazy?"

Instantly, everyone in the office stood up and started to pay attention to the kerfuffle.

"Crazy!?" Edward's voice trembled as he yelled. "You asshole! You're the one who gave me the date rape drug!" as he pushed Troy away so hard he stumbled back a few steps.

Troy adjusted his tie and tried to play it off as Judy and Daniel watched on in complete disbelief. "Uh, you must have me mistaken with someone else; you're not exactly my type, buddy." He mocked him.

Daniel suddenly clued in. "What? *This* is the guy from the Hallowe'en party?!" Then Judy was confused, "Can somebody please tell me what's going on here as she stepped forward to place her tiny body between them.

Edward piped up, trembling, "This fucktard tried to give a girl at the bar Rohypnol, but I drank it by mistake and then he and his goons beat me up." Troy looked nervous and tried to make Edward look foolish, but now everyone in the office had gathered and Troy's lip was quivering; he looked guilty. "What are you talking about? That's the stupidest thing I ever heard. Can we get security in here, please? By the way, you're fired, buddy!"

"I'm not your buddy," screamed Edward. "You're going down. You know who I am, and you know what you did, you pervert!" As Troy began to chuckle awkwardly, Edward leaped towards him with a clumsy right hook, and Troy went toppling backward in slow motion on to the desk behind him. Judy screeched again. "Edward! Stop!"

Troy held his jaw as he tried to get up off the desk. "You're asking for it now." He mocked Edward. It may have been meant as a threat but that's not how Edward took it; Edward dove over the table muttering a fusillade of barely intelligible curse words as he walloped Troy with punch after goofy punch.

Judy and others tried to pull them apart. Daniel, however, was cheering Edward on. "Dude, get him, get him!"

Judy was horrified, "Daniel, you're not helping! This is unacceptable! Edward, please stop!" But Edward couldn't stop. He'd never initiated a brawl in his life, and he didn't care that it was at work, or that he wasn't a very skilled fighter.

Edward was simply overcome with a sense of duty to pound Troy into the ground. Edward was unable to think of the consequences right now, even though everyone saw Edward lunge at Troy. With unwavering virtuousness, he knew he was defending the honour of the young lady Troy tried to drug.

The two squirmed around on the ground and Edward, having taken Troy by surprise, was clearly winning. "Rapist! You're a fucking rapist!" Edward made the crowd of onlookers gasp. People who worked with Edward began to realize that there was probably at least *some* truth to Edward's claims, as he had maintained the mildest of appearances for years!

The elevator doors opened and two security guards burst forth to break up the fight. They looked like referees breaking up a hockey brawl. Shirts askew, hair tousled, both were huffing and panting, and Troy's lip was bleeding.

Daniel tried to get close to Edward to fist bump him, but the security guard kept him at bay. "Please step back." Then to Troy, "Would you like us to call the police, Sir?"

Before Troy could respond, Edward blurted out, "Yes! Please, call the police because I have medical proof that he gave me Rohypnol!" The crowd gasped again in confusion.

"I didn't give *you* Rohypnol, Idiot!" Sneered Troy.

"Ah-ha! Did you hear that? He didn't give '*me*' Rohypnol, because it was meant for that girl at the Hallowe'en party!"

The security guards took both men by the arm into the elevator. "Look, we're going to have to get to the bottom of this. We're going to escort you both downstairs to the security office, and from there we'll decide what to do next."

Edward, Troy and the two guards entered the elevator as the entire office watched on silently with mouths gaping, except for Daniel who had managed to film some of it on his phone.

"I have to get this to Clotilde!" He muttered excitedly to himself as he nonchalantly attempted to walk back to his desk before sneaking downstairs to find Edward.

Everyone in the office was whispering because this was the last thing any of them expected to see on a Monday morning, with the least likely person instigating the incident. Theories were already getting thrown around, including, but not limited to conversations starting with, "Edward was so demure, he was bound to snap eventually" and "Edward's upset because his gay lover tried to drug him."

Then suddenly, Judy called out to Daniel, "Hey! Where do you think you're going?" Everyone else scurried back to their desks, but Daniel froze in his tracks and slowly, fearfully, turned around to face Judy.

"Uh... I was going to go back to work?" Daniel answered as if he was asking a question.

"Oh no you don't! I'm listening; what in the HELL was that all about? I have never seen Eddie act like that. Not anything *close* to that!" Whispered Judy loudly.

Daniel relaxed his stance and came up close to Judy, slouching a little and speaking softly as if to divulge a big secret. "Listen," his eyes shifted around the room to see if anyone was listening and he continued when he saw nobody was. "You remember seeing his eye last week; all beat up?"

Judy nodded and frowned simultaneously, confused but open to understanding. Despite witnessing Edward's attack on Troy, she was also very aware that this was extremely uncharacteristic behaviour on Edward's part and was willing to hear Daniel's take on the matter. "Yes, I saw— but what of it?"

"Well, I wasn't there, but—" Daniel stopped as Judy rolled her eyes. "I wasn't *there*, but I was *supposed* to be. If I *had been* there, probably none of this would have happened. Which, when you think about it, is better that we know what kind of douchebag this guy is rather than be unaware, don't you think?"

"How do we know he's a douchebag, Daniel?" Judy whispered impatiently and angrily.

"OK, so Edward and I were supposed to go to this Hallowe'en party at a club, except I had double booked myself and Edward had to go alone. Normally, he wouldn't do that. Anyway, he was at this club and got beat up by some random guy."

"And you think that was Troy?!" Blurted Judy in an even louder whisper.

"Well, I don't know, but Edward sure recognized him! I have never —and I mean *never*— saw him react like that to anyone or anything!" Daniel validated Edward's behaviour, and Judy had no choice but to visibly agree with the tilt of her head and rise of her eyebrows. "Go on," she said.

"So anyway, Edward started seeing this chick, who's a nurse who works with my sister and noticed how Edward has an unusually high alcohol tolerance, so how could he have gotten so drunk on one cocktail. I mean practically incapacitated, right? So this chick —"

Quite perturbed, Judy interrupted, "Say *'chick'* one more time and I'm going kick you in the shin!"

Daniel took a slight step back and continued more conscient-iously, enunciating every word, "This girl, I mean woman, *nurse*, said that he should get checked for Rohypnol. And as it turns out, he *did* have it in his system, but there was this group of girls at the club and it's most likely Edward accidentally took one of their drinks because the douchebag and all his douchey friends were hitting on them and pushed Edward out of the way. I'm not really sure *how* the fight started, but my boy doesn't get into fights!"

"OK, I think I'm following, but Troy didn't seem to recognize Ed at all."

"*Edward*, Judy; he likes to be called 'Edward' for god's sake. So yeah, he was wearing a costume, but the other guy was a just surfer, so I guess he was super easy for Edward to recognize." Daniel explained.

Judy contemplated these facts for a moment, wondering if they were indeed facts and was she understanding Daniel's version of events correctly. "OK, I'm down with what you're suggesting. Eddie, I mean, *Edward* has always appeared to be genuinely sweet and quiet, so it's really hard to believe he'd attack Troy, or anybody, for no reason."

"Exactly."

"The only thing we have to figure out is if Troy is actually the guy who beat him up and the person who gave him Rohypnol, or who accidentally gave it to him, intending it for some unsuspecting woman in the club."

They nodded at each other in agreement.

Judy's face took on a mischievous countenance. "Could you text me the name of the club, the date and time Edward would have been there, and a description of what he was wearing? I'm going to do a little investigating."

"Sure, thing! I'm on it." Daniel was finally able to relax. He continued to text his sister for Clotilde's number and went to the elevator.

Judy called after him, "And keep all these details to yourself, please, for now."

Daniel presumed she meant that he shouldn't discuss it with anyone in the office, but surely, Clotilde needed to know. "Yeah, no problem."

Meanwhile, Edward was sitting in the security office, with his forehead in his hand, embarrassed. The reality of what just happened was sinking in. He started to second-guess himself. Was Troy really the guy who beat him up? Troy was nowhere to be seen.

The security guard who had brought Edward downstairs, walked back into the small room and Edward immediately, nervously began to plead with him. "Hey, so is that guy going to press charges? I might have overreacted. Could I call someone? Don't I get a phone call?"

The security guard could see that Edward was very distressed, if not also remorseful. He kept his eyes fixed on Edward as he walked around the room but said nothing. Edward interpreted his behaviour as being smug, but in reality, the gentleman was simply curious, having just heard Troy's side of the story.

"Well?" Edward was becoming increasingly more upset. Two fights within days of each other, and now he could face criminal charges in addition to humiliating himself at the office!

"You're not in jail; you can call as many people as you'd like. Don't you have a cell phone on you?" The security guard was very matter-of-fact. Edward realized that he did have his phone on him, but had been so frazzled and worried about what would happen to him, that he completely forgot. "Yes... I do." He felt even more stupid.

The guard continued, "The gentleman has stated that he does not intend to press charges. However, there is still the matter of workplace aggression, or violence, in this particular case. HR is now involved, and as your current supervisor is technically a new-hire and on probation himself, it will come down to HR and your union rep deciding what to do with you."

Edward winced, turned and buried his head in his folded arms on the desk next to him. "I'm such an idiot! This is the dumbest thing I ever did." His muffled, sorrowful voice escaped from under his elbow.

The security guard managed to hear every word and pulled up a chair beside Edward. "Why don't you tell me what exactly happened," he said, calmly and compassionately. Edward slowly lifted his head, which was flushed, sweaty and possibly a little teary. Then Edward asked, "Well, what did Troy have to say?"

The guard shrugged. "Sorry, *that* I can't say. But I am interested in hearing what *you* have to say. You don't have to tell me, of course. I'm just supposed to keep you here until HR gives me further directives." He sat quietly with a sympathetic stare.

For some reason, Edward felt more relaxed with him now and decided that maybe he should get the saga off his chest one more time— especially the last bit. "OK, well, it all started when my friend Daniel and I decided to go to this Hallowe'en party at a nightclub," Edward told him the whole tale from beginning to end while the guard sat there with no visible reactions whatsoever. The less the guard emoted, the more Edward babbled; he found the guard very difficult to read.

Edward admitted, "You know, you could be an investigator; you don't show any emotional reaction to anything I'm saying." Then the guard got up and chuckled a brief but neutral "haha" but otherwise remained silent. Edward continued, "Yeah, like that." He paused and started up again, "Do you believe me? I am not the violent type at all. I didn't plan to hit the guy, you know? I didn't even know he was the guy until a few seconds before I swung at him. I even surprised myself. I just feel like a complete moron."

The guard squinted at him with a very slight smile, or what Edward thought was a smile. Then the guard started to talk slower somewhat under his breath, "You know, my daughter was a victim of a date rape drug." He peered into Edward's eyes. That's when Edward realized the guard hadn't been smiling at all; it was pain and anger he was trying to swallow.

They locked eyes for almost twenty-seconds. Edward waited patiently for him to continue but he didn't. "Did they catch the guy?" Edward was afraid to ask.

"No, they didn't." The guard gave him a deep blink that was almost audible. "If I had a chance to get my hands on him, though..." The guard stopped and began to fidget as he became visibly emotional and opted to shake his head and press his lips together rather than say another word.

Just then, the door opened, and an older stocky lady of ample proportion waddled in. She carried with her a file secured to a clipboard, and although she displayed an air of some authority, she also looked trepidatious walking into the narrow, overcrowded room with the two men. She cleared her throat excessively in preparation to identify herself as she straightened her heavy black-rimmed glasses.

"I'm Janet Leblanc from HR. I'm here to review the paperwork with you." Edward and the guard exchanged another couple of quick glances with each other. They didn't need to chat any further, because it was apparent to Edward what the guard was saying to him, if he, in fact, believed him, that Edward was justified in beating up a guy like that if Troy had actually spiked the drink with Rohypnol. The guard stood up, "He's all yours" and proceeded to walk out of the cramped office, leaving the door wide open.

Janet continued after she squished herself into the small desk chair and opened the file. "Your department head isn't pressing charges."

"You mean, *Troy*?" Edward was still perturbed by the automatic authority Troy was granted. "He's brand new; he's not even been here half a day!"

Janet tried to remain neutral. "I realize that, however, that *is* his position. The acting department head, Judy, has vouched for you, and as there were numerous witnesses, we're taking all that into account. I need you to fill out this paperwork which includes a recount of what happened, in your own words, and then this paper needs to be signed, in confirmation of your three-day suspension."

"Suspension!?" Edward exclaimed, making the lady jump. Now everyone seemed to be afraid of him. That wasn't something he wanted. He wasn't a guy that went around beating people up.

Janet nervously began to explain. "Yes," she cleared her throat again to anchor herself. "Suspended with full pay. It's to avoid any further altercations until we can make a decision. If we need more time, we'll extend your suspension."

"Wait. What? What kind of decision?" Edward's stomach was queasy.

"The decision to keep you on or terminate your employment," Janet said faintly, followed by an audible gulp.

Frustrated, Edward groaned loudly into the palms of his hands, "Good god, this is a nightmare! I can't believe this! What about him? Is Troy suspended?" He roared, and the guard slowly popped his head in Edward's line of sight, which made Edward realize the guard was listening to everything very closely.

"Sir, I understand how you must feel. But, no, he's not suspended." Janet couldn't wait to leave the room. "When you're done, with this paperwork, you can leave it here. Then the security guard will escort you and whatever personal belongings you have, out of the building until such time you're allowed to return." She swiftly swooshed between the desks and out of the office.

The guard returned with the door left open. Troy was seen walking past, arrogantly, as he was now allowed to return to their office upstairs. "I feel like crap," mumbled Edward.

Without realizing it, Edward let out a deep sigh and began to fill out the paperwork. He felt like he suddenly didn't know who he was anymore. Everything was shaken up; life used to be predictable, but right now, it was sheer chaos. One could argue that his attack on Troy was of his own doing and not activated by some force outside of himself. But to Edward, he couldn't believe that he reacted so instinctually, with barely any self-control.

Daniel could be heard in the other room, "Yeah, I went back up to get his stuff." He stated politely to the other guard. Edward was pleased to hear his voice and grateful Daniel was there to collect his belongings. "Just leave them here, please," requested the guard dryly.

Edward didn't want Daniel to go and was struck with a flash of panic. But Daniel piped in, "Could I just stay and wait for him?" There was a pause and then the guard said, "Sure; take a seat."

What a relief! He let out another deep sigh; Edward had no idea he had been holding his breath just then. He was very confused and felt like everything in his world was coming unglued. How could this happen? One moment, he was happily and imperviously floating through his days on a schedule with order, balance, and tranquillity. The next moment, he was having fights, dating a nurse, getting suspended from work. It was unheard of in the history of Edward.

CHAPTER SEVENTEEN

How hard does one's blood have to be pumping to be heard in one's own ears? Edward was not himself as he knew himself to be. Severe wooziness overtook him as he stood up to leave the tiny room with his paperwork. That's when Daniel spotted him. The look of distress on Daniel's face made Edward feel pitiful.

In a matter of minutes, which felt like seconds, Edward had handed over the papers, had collected his belongings from Daniel, put on his coat, and started out of the security area. No words exchanged between them until they were in the lobby.

His arms dangling by his side, shoulders slumped, and skin excessively dewy for this time of day, he peered woefully down at Daniel. "What the hell have I done, Daniel?"

"Dude, you're fine." Daniel tried to reassure him but didn't sound convincing, although he was very sincere. "You know, if you think about it, you've done a great thing. You just have to focus on the fact you know you did the right thing."

Edward felt worse. He wasn't sure that he had done the right thing at all. Surely, there could have been a better way to have handled it. And where did this uncontrollable impulse come from? Edward never felt like he repressed his anger; he just never really felt that angry. So it wasn't as if he had been suppressing his angry impulses for years and then they exploded. They just exploded on their own, or so he thought.

Any of the available options that could have been used, as Edward contemplated them in retrospect, would have been better than what he had done. He shuffled his feet across the lobby, put his gloved hands in his pocket. He was starkly different from the Edward who came in earlier that morning.

Suddenly Edward's phone started to vibrate, which startled him. He reached into his pocket to see who it might be, while Daniel stood quietly for one rare moment. He didn't know how to make his friend feel better.

"Hello?" Edward attempted to sound perky and pretend nothing was wrong when he answered the phone to speak to Clotilde. Daniel could hear her voice and then realized that perhaps he shouldn't have called her before Edward wanted her to know.

Edward slowly turned to glare at Daniel but kept talking to Clotilde.

"No, I'm fine. But I'm susp–" Edward was interrupted by Daniel's 'cut it' gesture across his throat.

Edward modified his words, "I'm supposed to go home while they figure things out here." He paused. "So Daniel texted you, eh?" He glared at Daniel.

Admittedly, Edward still felt horrible, but he was also comforted by the sound of Clotilde's voice. He walked away from Daniel, who didn't follow him for once. Daniel felt rather sheepish. Edward's natural lengthy stride was down to a mere shuffle, and his whole person was decreased.

The call ended once Edward was outside; he couldn't keep talking to Clotilde and not give away all the details. She was very supportive and told him she'd check in on him on her next break, but every kind gesture she put forth, only made Edward feel like a loser.

All the way home, Edward moped and didn't pay attention to where he was or how he moved through people and traffic. It was as if his body was on auto-pilot. Before he knew it, he was facing his apartment building and he had little recollection of how he arrived there. Every incident, every person, all the comments, the replay in his mind, contributed to his self-loathing mood.

How could a person who did everything right, who never hurt anyone, had the best intentions, never interfered with anything or anyone, who was content, fair, and humble— suddenly have this happen? As if the initial beating wasn't painful enough, now he actively, violently attacked the person he thinks beat him up. Not being in control of himself was worse than taking the humiliating beating. Having all his colleagues witness the assault, was even more devastating than that.

Sparky was very surprised to see Edward enter the apartment, and he meowed melodically as he watched his master throw his coat on the sofa and drop everything else on the table. He shuffled over to the sofa and flopped down across several seat cushions with a series of lamenting sighs. Sparky couldn't take much more of this and hopped onto Edward's chest, purring harshly while positioning himself in such a way that it made it more difficult for Edward to breathe.

Brooding was the order of the day. To compensate for Sparky's poor position, Edward stretched out while Sparky nestled into his master's sternum. Within minutes, Edward was asleep, his hand in mid-stroke on Sparky's back.

Sparky wasn't bothered by the full weight of Edward's arm on him. He could see Edward was upset and he revved up his purring once again, which lulled Edward into a deep, warm sleep. It was the kind of sleep that usually accompanies a cold or flu, almost fever-like.

While he slept, Edward's subconscious went into overdrive. How to heal and recover from this incident? How would this impact his career and his lifestyle? What if he had been more confrontational as a youth; would this have still happened? Was he actually a bad person who was just lying to himself for years?

Every neuron had been called to a general meeting, and electrical impulses were traveling back and forth inside Edward's brain far too intensely for him to be awake anyway. The multidimensional thought he was capable of while asleep was phenomenal. Usually, he didn't require this sort of thing for activities other than programming at work. Still, now this was a different type of "useful" automatic brain function, let alone an urgent situation.

The amount of stress he experienced that morning far out-weighed the cumulative stress of the past three decades of his life. As all the brain cells searched their files, admittedly, no, he had never felt this much stress, and as his walloped brain ran around in circles, it was evident that the last question needed to be answered first. If not, every morsel of memory that could float to the surface would be tainted with self-loathing. That has never helped anyone.

Was he actually a bad person who had been lying to himself for years? That was the big question, because that was the door that required opening and should it be a shoddy door that could easily become unhinged— indeed, everything was then unhinged.

All the parts of Edward's psyche, his various brain vassals, came up to report with unshakable evidence and presented it to his sovereign mainframe that would hopefully carry this news forward to his waking consciousness. There was no incident of Edward harming people or animals, whether accidental or intentional, as far back as they were able to access.

Edward's mind was splitting into archetypal versions of himself and each one had a different perspective. The common thread was that Edward wouldn't mistreat a soul until The Cynic showed up and posed the question, "What if you're *all* biased?" the voice of self-doubt proclaimed dryly. "You're all just parts of Edward; you could be lying to him too."

Flustered, the rest of Edward's brain scurried around preparing its rebuttal, because as was often the case, the voice of the cynic was louder and more influential that the entire cluster of reasonable facts. However, in the end, no— the collective decided that they could stand by their deposition with solid examples of Edward's entire life. The cynic wasn't impressed but gave in with a less than rousing, "Whatever."

Then the cynic sat quietly for some time. The remainder of Edward's brain rested momentarily. The Philosopher sided with the cynic and proposed an idea, "If Edward was proven simply, not to *be a bad person*, is he automatically awarded 'good person' status?" Edward's brain started buzzing again. Arguments rushed back and forth, such as, "If the world were full of Edwards, we'd be living in a much nicer place!"

It was something they could all agree on, but then Childhood Memory popped up and said, "If I may just bring one small item to your attention. I can recall a few things that you might have forgotten. Let me preface that with the notion that we don't *fondly remember* the people or situations that merely didn't harm us." Edward's brain froze for a second. "Sure, there were many incidents you all have presented that prove Edward isn't a bad person."

"Until punching Troy in the face, Edward never stood up for a damn thing." A profound sense of peace washed over the entirety of Edward's mind, and subsequently, his body. It sunk in. Passive contentment was akin to obliviousness. Ignorance may be bliss, but does it help anyone else? It was unanimously decided upon, even the cynic agreed, that this was a critical turning point in Edward's inert existence.

Then as if a series of alarms had been set-off, Edward began to stir. He was vibrating, and with a jolt, he sat up, unaware of where he was or what was happening. He suddenly remembered he was at home and why, and then realized it was his phone vibrating and ringing. It was Clotilde.

A groggy, soft, "Hey..." was all Edward could muster at first.

Clotilde assumed he was in a deeply depressed state and proceeded with caution, "Any news?" She asked, almost whispering?

Edward sensed her tone and cleared his throat, "No, no, I've been sleeping all this time."

"Ever since you got home?"

"Yeah..." There was silence. Clotilde didn't know what to offer Edward in the way of consolation. "How are you feeling about things?"

Edward cleared his throat again, trying to sound more like himself. "You know, I'm actually ok."

"Really?" Asked Clotilde, somewhat unconvinced.

"Yeah, I think so. When I think about it, honestly, I know that was the guy who beat me up, and he or one of his friends spiked the drink. I'm not sorry. Maybe I overreacted, but I've never been in a situation like that before and really, how was I supposed to react?" Edward's subconscious thoughts had made their way to the foreground. It was wonderful.

Clotilde was relieved to hear the confidence in Edward's voice. "Wow, you sound very different from just a few hours ago!"

"A few hours? How long have I been sleeping?"

"It's almost one o'clock in the afternoon..." Clotilde informed him.

"Holy shit, I was totally knocked out. I never felt so exhausted." Edward was perplexed at how that morning's events had hit him. Sparky sat like a tea cozy on the upper ledge of the sofa, squinting at him.

"I have to get back to work, but I'm glad you sound better. Let me know if you hear anything." Clotilde said, warmly. Edward was pleased he could hear the smile in her voice again.

"I'm going to text Daniel to see what the climate in the office is like right now."

The call ended and Edward sat up, put his feet firmly on the ground. He stretched his neck, shoulders, and arms in every direction. Sparky was mildly impressed; he'd never really seen Edward try to move like him.

Just as Edward stood up, a call was coming in. Edward chuckled to himself, "Daniel, you're hilarious." But it wasn't Daniel; it was Judy. Butterflies instantly returned to Edward's stomach.

"Hello?" Edward said firmly yet cautiously. Fortunately, Judy only heard the confidence in Edward's voice and also was trying to be supportive or decent at the very least. "Hi, Ed– Edward. It's Judy. I have intel for ya."

"Intel?" Edward asked, genuinely surprised by her choice of words.

"Yes, did you file a report yet?"

Confused by her question, Edward responded, "A report? Like with the cops?"

"Yeah, like with the cops." Judy snapped back. "I called the bar where you allegedly got beat up. They do actually have security cameras, and they keep the footage for two weeks before it automatically gets deleted. They don't generally look at the footage, they said, unless something happens. Apparently, the place is prone to bar fights for whatever reason and so they had cameras installed earlier this year."

"Allegedly? I *was* beaten up." Edward felt the need to insist upon that key point before addressing the rest of Judy's news.

"Ok, you were. But, let's see who did it." Judy calmed herself again. "They volunteered to either send us a copy or if there was a file number with the police, they would send it to them. I told them I'd contact you first. It's going to have to come from you."

Edward felt both elated that he could possibly have indisputable proof, although he didn't want to get his hopes up and was also comforted that Judy had faith in him to try and get to the bottom of things.

"Well, I guess I know what my next step is; I'll head over to the police station right now," Edward spoke confidently.

"Cool. Then get that file number over to the bar asap so that they can send the footage." Judy sounded like she was orchestrating a covert mission.

Edward ended the call, but it wasn't easy for him to stay calm. He didn't want to get ahead of himself. What if the footage was blurry or unclear? What if the view of Troy's face was obstructed? He knew not to get too excited until the proof was apparent to everyone.

This was definitely a step in the right direction, and above everything else, Edward was most pleased with the fact Judy was helping. All these years, Edward felt that his only real friend was Daniel, and even though he hadn't had negative experiences with others, he never had people he could rely on or who he felt would go to bat for him. It was a refreshing change.

Immediately, Edward found the paper from the clinic and proceeded to the police station. His step was bright and perky again— as much as it could be for a man. He was feeling reenergized. He bounded on to the curbs and practically leapt off of them. He was feeling so positive. He arrived at the police station and then had to figure out his way to the correct wicket.

Fortunately, there was an information desk that he had to check into first. He explained to the lady that he wished to file a report against somebody who assaulted him. Edward was issued a number on a flimsy stub of paper and was told to take a seat in the waiting room. It was almost as bad as the emergency room as he scanned the occupants. All the normal, sane people were congregating at one end of the room while the shady characters were at the other end. There was a TV looming above on the long wall broadcasting the news channel with closed captioning across it.

Edward didn't think that was the best choice of programming, considering the clientele. He would have picked something more lighthearted like cartoons. He sat down in the sane-people-section and looked up at the electronic number board. There were several types of numbers on display and they were at C-39. Edward's ticket said C-41, which was a relief. He estimated that his wait would not be too long after all, as there was only so long that he could refrain from making eye-contact with the less sane people in the room.

He pulled out his phone and sent texts to both Clotilde and Daniel, informing them, each in their own style, about what was going on. Then Edward preoccupied himself with game after game of solitaire.

With each 'ding' of the numbers changing on the overhead screen, Edward would glance up just long enough to see the first letter of the sequence; if it were anything but a "C", he would instantaneously resume his game. Then within minutes, "C-41" popped up. Edward slipped his phone in his pock and proceeded to the appropriate wicket.

A young, fair-skinned man with cropped, curly, red hair was waiting to serve him. "Hello, what can I do for you today?" He chimed to Edward. It sounded more like a barista taking an order than a clerk at the police station.

"Well. Let's see, so I was assaulted on the evening of Hallowe'en at a party at a nightclub. As it turns out, the guy who beat me up might also have accidentally given me Rohypnol and—"

The clerk straightened up and dropped the tone of his voice down a notch. "What? Someone 'accidentally' gave you—"

"Yeah; I think it was meant for the girls next to me, and I accidentally took the drink." Edward clarified.

"Ok, go on." The clerk was intrigued and listened with his brow furrowed.

Edward continued. "Anyway, yeah, I have the urine test that shows it and also the nightclub said they have the incident recorded, and if I file the report here and then give them the file number, they'll send you guys the footage."

The clerk was somewhat perplexed but intrigued. "Okay..." he mumbled slowly. "Could I see that paper, please?" Edward slipped the folded paper under the glass through the tray towards the clerk who quickly took it and skimmed it. He continued, "And do you happen to know the identity of the person who assaulted you?"

Edwards's eyebrows bounced up and his eyes opened wide. "Funny you should ask. As it turns out, I went into work today and my new department head, who just started this morning, just so happens to be the guy." Edward's expression looked like, "What do ya think of that!" and the clerk responded accordingly. "Are you serious?" he whispered in astonishment. "Did you confront him at all?"

"Confront? Yeah, you could say that." Edward tried to avoid this particular detail but the clerk waited, blinking at him as he typed the details into his computer until Edward volunteered more information.

"Yeah, I decked him." Edward sighed embarrassedly.

"Meaning? You assaulted him? How? Verbally? Physically punched...?"

"I don't think I said anything, but yes, I punched him." Edward felt like a Neanderthal.

"OK. Were there witnesses?" The clerk tried to remain neutral.

"Yes, my entire office, my best friend, my manager."

"Could you give us names and phone numbers of at least two primary witnesses."

Edward gave him all the details, including his own address, phone number, and all the other information he required. The clerk read it all back to him and sent him a copy via email. "In the email I just sent you, you'll see the case number and the officer in charge of looking into the file. Do you have any questions?"

Edward was impressed with the ease and efficiency of the whole process and thought for a second. "No, I think that pretty much does it. Thank you."

The clerk pressed out an awkward smile that was more like an attempt to conceal a smirk, and then added, "If you need to add anything or want to check on the status, you can call the main number and quote your case number, and someone will fill you in."

Now it was a matter of sitting at home and patiently waiting. Edward turned around and walked briskly to the main doors. He decided to text Judy before heading out. He sent her the file number and told her they'd probably contact her to get her take on what happened. She replied almost instantly and said she'd forward the file number to the guy she spoke with at the nightclub. Edward was genuinely grateful.

One minute, he was just an insignificant, anonymous computer geek who still felt more like a boy than a man most of the time. Then suddenly, his life involved barroom brawls, fistfights, police, sex, and drugs. Edward was flabbergasted. He didn't feel as pathetic as he did earlier, nor was he afraid of what would happen to himself. Having taken the appropriate steps, he felt like justice would prevail.

On the way home, Edward received a text message from Daniel.

It read, "Dude. Cops just showed up to question Troy. He's not taking it well. Holy..."

Edward began to get slightly more nervous. What if this questioning infuriated Troy, and he decided to come after him? He texted a reply to Daniel, "OK, good, what's he saying tho?"

Daniel texted back, "He's swearing to the cops!! Making a HUGE fuss!" Edward was becoming increasingly anxious. Daniel texted again, "Shit. Dude. They are taking him out."

"Taking him out?!" Edward wasn't sure what Daniel meant.

"Taking Troy with them." Daniel reverted to plain English.

"OK," Edward was somewhat relieved by that.

However, when Edward arrived home, he realized he was agitated and flustered. The impatience tingling around the small of his back made its way down his gangly legs forcing him to take up pacing as if it were an Olympic sport. He walked down the hall, looked out the window, walked back, circled the living room, went to the bathroom, emptied his bladder more frequently than usual and continuously grumbled. Sparky stared at him disapprovingly.

Then Edward started to speak aloud to himself while pacing. He became so self-absorbed with his overwrought monologue that he almost sprung to the ceiling when his phone rang. Panting, he ran to the phone and uttered a weak and breathless, questioning "hello?" as he didn't even bother to see if he knew the number on the screen.

It was the police. Edward gulped as he heard the deep, authoritative voice state, "This is Constable Sanderson. Is this Edward?" Even though Edward felt that the police officer was totally hamming up the tone of his voice to sound intimidating, it was still working.

"Yes, this is Edward." In his attempt to sound unfazed, he instead sounded cocky and obnoxious, which wasn't at all what he was going for. He could feel himself recoil as Constable Sanderson made a throat-clearing sound that obviously expressed the fact he was not impressed. Edward made a quick recovery by repeating what he just said a level lower on the assertive scale.

The constable continued, "We've already received the digital security files of the nightclub you frequented on October thirty-first." There was a lengthy pause because Edward assumed he would continue on his own, but he didn't. Cumbersomely, Edward asked, "Oh? And what did you see there?" He felt particularly daft.

The constable was enjoying making Edward squirm. "It appears to be that the individual in the footage is the same person you identified at your workplace earlier today. With the additional evidence we have been able to acquire from the security footage, we are proceeding to arrest this individual on a variety of charges, most of which I am not at liberty to discuss with you. However, he will not be returning to your workplace for the time being."

Edward stood in his living room, flabbergasted with his mouth gaping. "Thank you. That's really efficient of you." He still sounded cheeky, but he was actually sincere.

The constable gave Edward a few additional details about the process and that he would have to submit an affidavit within a few days. Then he would be notified of a court date where he would have to testify. That last bit of news almost made Edward just about drop his intestines on the floor. But, it was better than the alternative, which was being charged with assault himself, and not being able to return to work. Which reminded him, "What about my job? Can I go back to work then?"

"Sir, I'm assuming that's something you'll have to take up with human resources at your place of employment."

"Yes, of course. Sorry." This guy made Edward feel like an imbecile. He quickly thanked him again and got off the phone. He started jumping up and down, shouting, "Yes! Yes! Yes!" while punching his fists up in the air, and prancing back and forth, then quickly had to check that he did actually hang up. He didn't need to be humiliated any further and continued silently dancing.

Edward was elated, and yet there was a part of him that was worried about what would happen between now and the court date. That could be months from now and he imagined having to hideout or look over his shoulder every time he went out. What if Troy was able to find out where he lived? What if he got his friends to go after him? Edward's peace of mind was short-lived, but he endeavoured to focus on the better news and not the potential for disaster.

As he found himself pacing once again, his phone rang and startled him a second time. It was Judy.

"Hello." Answered Edward breathlessly but overall pleased with the latest developments.

"Hey, Edward. I guess you heard; they arrested Troy."

"Yeah, I just talked to the cops."

"Pretty wild. See you back at work tomorrow." There was a distinct, recognizable warmth to Judy's voice, which made Edward feel very appreciated, for once.

The day's events progressed at a speed that baffled Edward. It was only a few hours ago that he flung himself through the air to punch and tackle his new department head to the floor. Not as surprising was that it was followed by his suspension, getting escorted out of his beloved workplace, visiting the police station with his evidence, security footage corroborating his story, which led to Troy getting arrested. Life boomeranged with a call from Judy welcoming him back to work tomorrow. Who was this guy? Whose life was this?

"I think I'll have a beer, Sparky." Edward scratched the cat's head, not nearly long enough for Sparky, who then let out a snappy meow that most likely was a feline swear word as Edward turned to the fridge.

There's nothing quite like the rewarding sound of a cold can of beer being cracked open when you really need one. Edward was so pleased with himself he felt like a superhero. Not a buff superhero full of finesse and pizazz, of course, but the scrawny underdog type.

CHAPTER EIGHTEEN

As far back as Edward could remember, Tuesdays were always agreeable days, but today was one of the sweetest Tuesdays of all time. As he went through his tried and true morning routine, there was a lightness in his thoughts, a flutter in his heart, and a skip in his step. He wasn't what you'd call a *great* dancer, but he could keep a rhythm, and he was inarguably fluid. Edward cavorted throughout the apartment to whatever tunes were playing on the radio. As usual, Sparky was ashamed by this display, although he'd grown quite accustomed to feeling this way about Edward. He pitied him.

"Hey, Sparky boy! Today is a very good day! It's a great day!" He growled out the word 'great,' and Sparky rolled his eyes. He just wanted to be fed and could do without Edward's galloping about.

Edward topped Sparky's kibble, as he sashayed across the kitchen floor. Sparky was happy to bury his face in the dish and not have to be subjected to one more second of this halfwitted performance.

The text messages were coming in from Daniel and Clotilde while Edward made his way to work. They were welcomed because Edward was getting nervous despite everything seeming to have wrapped up well the previous day. He was worried that people at work would only remember his maniacal behaviour and was embarrassed. The plan, as he informed Daniel, was to sneak onto the floor and slip down the last row to his cubicle where he would stay for the entire day.

Not that it was a good disguise or even a disguise at all, Edward had his scarf up over his chin and the lapels of his wool coat pulled up towards his ears as he stealthily floated across the lobby floor to the elevators, keeping his gaze down to shoulder height. It was as effective as when Sparky would attempt to conceal himself under the sofa; everything but his head was exposed, and there was no mistaking him.

Daniel appeared out of nowhere, looking back to see if anyone noticed him. "Dude." He whispered with a nod.

Edward barely made eye contact, and nodded back. They stood close together, not uttering a word, awaiting the elevator. No familiar faces were standing anywhere near them. The elevator arrived and the huddled crowd moved onboard in unison. Periodically Daniel and Edward would glance at each other, their eyes filled with commentary that neither of them actually understood.

Only four people remained when the elevator reached their floor. The doors slid open, and Edward and Daniel stepped out. Within seconds of the doors closing behind them, just as they turned around to make their way to their respective cubicles, a spontaneous round of applause came from five or six people scattered about the front section of the office floor. Edward was stunned. He was utterly immobilized; still, with his snug-fitting scarf and elevated lapels, he needed a moment to realize people were actually reaffirming his actions and were praising him.

Both he and Daniel slowly turned to see where the clapping was coming from. A young man standing in front of the second desk, whose name Edward didn't even know, came at him with his hand out to congratulate him rather exuberantly. "Awesome move yesterday, Edward! You rock!" Edward's arm almost got shaken off at the hinges. He glared at Daniel and pushed his chin up over the scarf and then pulled the scarf down with his free hand. There was obviously no need for the disguise.

"No worries, man," Edward said to the fellow as he snatched his hand back. He glanced around the room and saw the smattering of his other early-bird colleagues smiling and nodding in support. Edward was perplexed and quickly turned back to his set path, directly to his cubicle with Daniel.

As soon as they arrived there, they both hung up their coats as quickly as they could, sat down in their chairs, and swivelled backwards to the aisle to chat.

"What the hell?" Whispered Edward, looking to Daniel for a viable explanation.

Daniel continued to look back over his shoulders before speaking, "Don't ask me. It's weird. It's not like I personally disagree with what you did; I think it's totally deserved. But these guys?" He waved his index finger around, meaning 'everyone in the entire office'. "They are so frikkin' straight-laced and don't even know the whole story!"

Edward shrugged spastically with disbelief. Daniel threw his hands up to match him and raised him a series of head shakes. "And who was that guy?!" Whispered Daniel as loud as he could while still being considered whispering.

"Yeah, Ok! I thought it was just me! You don't know him either? Geez, man. This is so weird. Item #167 on the list of things no one would ever expect to happen to me." Edward was more confused than he'd ever been, and with the unfolding of recent events, that really said something.

The pair had no resolution to their quandary and mutually decided to simply focus on their work. Edward started up his computer in the way he'd done every morning since he started there. It took no time at all before he became fully engrossed in his coding.

Mere moments later, he finally forgot about the incident; Judy appeared out of nowhere while Edward's defences were down. "Hey!" She announced!

Edward's limbs jolted out from all sides. "Hi... Judy," he yelped unexpectedly like a prepubescent boy with voice cracking special effects and all. Judy chuckled.

"Nice to have you back, Ed." Judy fell back into her old habit but quickly corrected herself as she could feel Daniel glaring at her. "Edward, we're all behind you here. I can't believe what they've got on this guy."

Edward and Daniel wheeled closer with their chairs. "What do you mean?" asked Edward as he felt he was about to be filled in on some top-secret information.

"You didn't hear?" Judy asked, surprised.

Both Daniel and Edward swivelled up even closer to Judy. They admitted they hadn't heard anything more. Then Edward said, "Except, the cops did say they were arresting him on multiple charges, but couldn't tell me what."

Judy's eyes got wider. "Yeah, so when I was talking with the bar manager, who happened to be there early yesterday because they were doing some repairs on bar taps. He went to look for the footage right away, but then he called me back later and I guess then informed the police of everything. The guy got all curious and started looking at other days because he noticed Troy looked familiar. He found actual footage of him putting something in a girl's drink from the night before!"

Edward and Daniel let out a symphonic, "Whoa!" in stereo. Judy continued, "Yeah, and as this was 'his new employer' enquiring, the manager felt like it was his duty to inform me."

Edward raised his eyebrows, "You're his employer?"

"So I stretched the truth!" Judy was impressive with her skills. Daniel and Edward were very surprised but pleased to hear about this enlightening development and also that Judy was so keen to let them in on the inside scoop.

The three of them shared a round of satisfied grins. "Ok, get back to work!" Judy said as she happily waltzed away. Daniel couldn't hold his tongue one second more, "Oh my god, dude! Dude!" Edward replied, "I know! I know!" The two of them were ecstatic, but they both quickly decided to get back to work, hold off on the full extent of their jubilation, and make the best of the day now that they knew for certain Troy really had it coming to him.

Edward became so profoundly enthralled with his work that he didn't notice lunchtime sneak up on him. He no longer felt the need to hide, and a sense of peace and calm washed over him.

He felt like what had happened over the past several days was almost a dream. It was so far out of the realm of normal that he genuinely had a difficult time accepting it as real.

Then he found himself reminiscing about the evening he spent with Clotilde. Was this the new Edward? Edward 2.0? Alternate Universe Edward with a girlfriend, a sex life, defender of the innocent, barroom brawler; what else could he expect from this new persona? Sparky was consistent and so was Daniel. Edward wasn't sure what to think or how to classify these changes.

Just then, Clotilde called, knowing that it was probably Edward's lunch break. She was delighted to know he was just thinking about her and he was delighted that he could be open and honest enough to tell her that he was— as surprising as it all still was to him. Edward really was different from how he'd been previously, and the sudden shift was not yet feeling natural. It was as if his life had started on a new path all on its own, and Edward's body was going through the motions as it was programmed to, but his mind and his personality were playing catch-up. It was a peculiar situation.

So as to not take up too much time out of Edward's lunch break, Clotilde suggested they get a late dinner after her shift to celebrate Edward's return to work and Troy's arrest. Edward was all for it and felt slightly giddy with optimism. After hanging up with Clotilde, Daniel peeked around the cubicle wall, having heard the whole conversation, and said in a somewhat pleased but teasing fashion, "Oh, so you're like the big hero now, eh? Going on a Tuesday night date. Look at you!"

With his head tilted down, Edward peered back at Daniel with his eyeballs almost pressed up against his eyebrows. "Please stop."

"C'mon, let's go eat." Daniel was truly happy for Edward and enjoyed seeing how flustered he could make him. Daniel knew something had changed in Edward, but he also didn't understand the depth of the transformation.

As they went to eat lunch, other office workers stared at Edward slightly longer than usual but nobody engaged him in conversation. Other than the initial cheering that occurred first thing in the morning, everybody else tried to behave like normal and not make a fuss over Edward so as not to intentionally make him feel uncomfortable.

Edward wasn't sure what was worse. Part of him wanted to talk about it; he wanted to make sure people knew why he did what he did and didn't want anyone to be afraid of him or feel that he acted irrationally or without cause. On the other hand, he wanted his experience within the office to be just as it was before. The one thing Edward was deeply satisfied with was the level of acknowledgment and assistance he received from Judy. She no longer made him feel stupid, foolish, or inadequate —not to mention, unliked!

Lunch break continued and it made Edward feel increasingly more normal, at least comfortable with its predictability. Despite that, something was nagging at Edward, just under the surface. He couldn't address it yet, as he wasn't fully aware that it existed for one, but also he didn't know how to begin to approach the topic with himself or even how to bring it to the surface. So for the time being, the entire nagging subject was postponed.

The day progressed, much like it would have any other Tuesday. Nobody bothered with Edward and he was content with that. He thought that maybe he should tell his parents about what happened now that there was some sort of resolution and they wouldn't have to worry. He wasn't overly close to his parents in a way that they shared interests or deep conversations. Still, he had what would be considered a healthy, functional relationship with them, based on a relatively positive and uneventful childhood. It was decided; he would call them when he returned home.

It wasn't all that difficult to stay focused on the day's tasks; once Edward was deep in his coding, that was ample motivation to adhere to the job at hand. What Edward seemed to be contemplating in the cozy nooks of his somewhat subconscious mind, was that despite the difficulties of the bizarre situations that had arisen of late, the ease at which they were resolved was just as unexpected. It wasn't only their favourable resolution that he questioned, but it was the speed at which everything returned to normal. The baseline for what was now considered normal, however, had also changed in the process.

At any moment, Edward was expecting the universe to snap back into place, causing every milligram of progress he'd made to revert to the previous benchmark for 'normal' that he was used to experiencing over the course his entire life. That was something else he didn't understand yet but he would learn eventually. Once a change like this occurred, there was no 'bouncing back'; the universe was changed forever and what was happening was real and had different consequences.

It was as simple as that. One shift in the past pattern and the outcome changed. As Edward contemplated before, was that destiny? Was that his designed trajectory *correcting* itself? Was he hoping to awaken behaviours that remained relatively dormant for his whole life prior to that? Did some predetermined impetus occur *because* he was dormant? Was there a failsafe mechanism in place that said, "Should Edward not do or be such and such by this date, introduce 'Event B' AKA: getting beat up at the Hallowe'en party"?

Who really knew what the impetus was. Perhaps it was Daniel not going to the party, and Edward was compelled to go on his own. There could have been numerous more subtle incidents that occurred along the way that Edward missed, and that's why it took such a violent act to snap him into place.

The indisputable fact was that Edward always exhibited far less than what he had going for himself. Humility was an outstanding quality to have, but in Edward's case, he wasn't even aware that he needed to be humble about anything. He always somehow felt that he was a mere peasant among kings.

When someone has so many inherent gifts yet doesn't choose intentionally, but rather accidentally, to act without greed, pride, or arrogance, then an abrupt remedy was indeed required. Edward was an exceptional human being, even just considering things from a physical specimen standpoint. He was taller than average, towering over his peers actually, and handsome, bright, articulate, intuitive, righteous, unbiased, amiable, dignified, lighthearted, financially stable, and chivalrous! His fault, if he had one that loomed over all the others, was simply that he didn't have a clue that he was magnificent in any way at all.

By the time Edward reached his apartment, Clotilde had texted twice with contradicting information. Her first text suggested meeting at a restaurant shortly after 7 PM, somewhere near the hospital. In the second text, she said she was getting off work about half an hour early and could meet at home instead if he wanted.

Edward thought about it for a moment and uncharacteristically came up with a third option. He searched the internet with his phone looking for restaurants near the hospital. He found one that was a step or two up from the pub atmosphere he would typically default to and then texted Clotilde with the suggestion for a meeting time of 6:45. That would give him enough time to call his parents, feed Sparky, leave, and get there on time.

Sparky was staring at Edward as if he could see the wild, electric thoughts blitz around his head in a tapestry of feline-visible colours. Edward noticed for a change. "What's up, Sparky? You're looking at me funny." Sparky meowed his hungry meow because he didn't know how to explain to Edward what he was really thinking. Even if he did, it would be wasted on Edward's limited vocabulary. "You want food, don't ya?" was Edward's interpretation.

They walked to the kitchen and Sparky wove his steps synchronistically between Edward's feet; he always thought he would step on him, but he never did. "I know, I know, you're hungry. I'm going to go eat with Clotilde tonight." The last bit of information was irrelevant to Sparky. Once the bottom of his dish was covered, and there was no risk of the bowl not being filled by the next time it was bare, there was nothing else for Sparky to care about.

Edward fed him and awaited Sparky's purring gratitude and then made his way around the apartment, closing curtains, changing the channel on the tv, checking to see if Clotilde had texted back (she hadn't), sat down on the sofa and then called his parents' house. They were some of the few people he could think of that still had a landline.

The phone rang three times before his dad picked up; they had call display, so he knew it was Edward calling. "Hey, Edward. You just caught us." His dad said rather jovially.

"Oh, hey. Why? What's up?" Edward was mildly surprised by his father's upbeat tone.

"We're just heading out to dinner before a show. I got these tickets from a colleague who can't make it. Your mother's always saying we should partake in activities like this, and now look at what she's manifested!"

"Manifested?" Edward hadn't ever heard his father use that word in this context before. Then he could hear his mother speaking in the background. "What's she saying?" He asked.

"Here." Edward's dad passed the phone to his wife. "Hello, Edward. How's everything? Could we call you back later tonight? Is that going to be too late?" She was a pleasant-sounding woman, motherly yet not at all naive.

"Uh, no, it's not too late. Well, how late do you mean?" Edward answered the last question first.

"Well, you know, it might be too late for *us*. It *is* a school night!" She chuckled. They'd been saying, "school night" for as long as Edward could remember. "Is everything all right? You don't usually call on a Tuesday." Her intuition was correct.

"All right? Well, yeah, it is now." He said, not meaning to start down that road if they were heading out and didn't have time for the whole story.

"What happened?" His mom asked, evidently concerned.

"Oh, it's a long story, but everything's ok now." He tried to sound reassuring.

Then he could hear his dad ask if something was wrong as he was picking up on the concern in his wife's voice. "What happened?"

"He's ok, he said," repeated his mother to answer his father, but then continued at Edward, "Now you have me wondering, though; are sure you're all right?"

Edward didn't want them to be late. "Yes, yes, it's kind of a funny story, in retrospect. I'll catch up with you later."

"Well, do you want us to pick you up? You could come with us to dinner." She asked, still notably worried to a lesser degree.

"No, no— you guys go out on your date. Actually, I'm going on a date too." Edward hoped that would lighten the mood. He really would have preferred to tell his story from start to finish, but talking to his parents never went according to plan, and now they were getting all the shocking headlines with no details and no context.

"You mean with a girl?" His mother sounded genuinely shocked.

Mildly offended, Edward replied, "Yes, with a girl! Seriously?"

His mother laughed, "I didn't mean it like that. What does she do, this girl?"

His father could be heard in the background, "What girl?" and his mother replied, "He's going on a date."

"Ok, mom, mom—" Edward tried to get his mom's attention; he sincerely didn't want his parents to be late for their evening out. "She's a nurse and—" he was cut off again because his mother was relaying the information back to his father, who then replied, "A nurse? That's handy."

"Guys, don't you have a speakerphone? I don't want you to be late on my account."

"Edward, your father and I aren't 'guys.'" His mother said sternly.

"Well, I am." Piped in his father. Then the speaker feature was turned on. "OK, Edward, you're on the loudspeaker now; go on." Continued his mother. "Did you hear that? Your father says he *is* a guy."

"Yes, I heard." Edward shook his head as this conversation was unraveling quicker than he could say 'you guys' one more time. "Look, why don't you go out, enjoy yourselves, see your show, and we'll talk later."

"OK, well, we have you on speaker now, and you won't talk. Are you going to be around later tonight?" asked his mother. It wasn't always easy to navigate her.

Edward was getting frustrated, "Yes, but I might be here with Clotilde."

His mother was still probing, "On a *first* date? What kind of girl is this?"

Then his father interrupted, "Maybe it's *not* a first date. Is that her name?"

Edward was now regretting, even attempting this conversation. "Yes, of course it's her name."

His mother continued, "Well, what kind of girl goes to a strange man's apartment on a first date?"

"Who are you calling a *strange man*?" Asked Edward and his father in unison.

Edward started speaking over them both, "Mom, mom, listen. It's not the first date. Her name is Clotilde. She's a nurse. She works with Daniel's sister at the hospital. She's very nice. Really, very nice and—" Edward softened up as he started thinking about how truly wonderful Clotilde was and that 'nice' didn't even begin to describe her. He punctuated the sentence with a big sigh.

Then his father asked cheekily, "Is she a French girl, Edward? That's a French name, isn't it?"

Edward rubbed his forehead and closed his eyes. There was no way to tell his story in any ordinary fashion. "Yes, I suppose it is."

"Your father's raising and lowering his eyebrows— *repeatedly*! Well, I'm sure she's lovely, Edward, and I didn't mean to say you're strange. I was just— you know, generalizing. I can't wait to hear all about her. We'll try you later, and if you're busy, well... well, you just call us back whenever." She stumbled on the word "busy" as it she realized it could mean so many things.

"OK, bye. I'll catch you later. Have fun!" Edward desperately wanted to end the call.

"Bye, Edward!" both parents sang the words together and hung up.

After twisting and cracking his neck on both sides, releasing a hefty amount of tension that had so rapidly accumulated, Edward said aloud with another deep sigh, "What the hell?! Oh god, I hope they don't call back tonight." He then realized he was still waiting for Clotilde.

"Yes!" He exclaimed as he checked his messages. Clotilde had responded with a, "Sounds good. C U soon!"

Edward started skipping, in his own manly way, around the room. Maybe this was why his mother asked if he was going on a date with a girl. He paused briefly and changed his stride to something exaggeratedly macho. It really didn't suit him. Sparky had emerged from the kitchen and was once again embarrassed at this almost obscene display by his master.

"Hey, Sparky, can you see me like this? Imagine I was this macho. Maybe this is the new me." He thrust his bony pelvis forward and cupped his crotch, mocking a gangster he saw on television. In his best New York gangster accent, he pretended to speak to someone who was not there, "Eh... don't you mess with me, or I'll kick your ass!" Sparky ran away and hid. As far as he was concerned, this was uncalled for and completely out of hand.

But Edward continued and proceeded to make fake karate moves in slow motion with all the ridiculous sound effects. Then with a speedy wind-up of his hands, he funnelled the energy into his leg and swiftly kicked the coffee table with his ankle.

Immediately, Edward crumbled to the floor, writhing in agony, beaten by a piece of stationary furniture, he muttered, "Mo*ther* fu —!!". He was in too much pain to even complete the word.

Squeezing out a series of grunts, Edward finally spoke: "Oh my god, I'm so stupid." Seated on the carpet, he pulled up his pant leg and pushed down his sock. "Holy!" He yelped. His ankle was swelling up before his eyes. He cautiously hopped up, trying not to walk on that *particular* foot as much as the unbeaten one, and waddled to the kitchen, whispering with great urgency, "Ice, ice, ice. Edward, you're an idiot."

Edward flung open the freezer door, grabbed a lunchbox ice pack, and shoved it down his sock. "Oh, that's cold." He stood there until he couldn't tolerate the sensation any further. Sparky had reemerged; he could no longer ignore the bewildering babbling of his master. As curiosity would have customarily killed the cat— Sparky was unimpressed and upset that he had come all the way out for this. He returned to Edward's room and hid under the bed indefinitely.

Suddenly, Edward realized he needed to hurry up for his date. He could feel his ankle stinging and throbbing intermittently. It was likely not a severe injury, just a moronic one. It was enough for Edward to realize that he shouldn't become too full of himself; perhaps he hadn't changed as much as he thought. He was still, essentially Edward, the same Edward he always was but maybe steps closer to self-actualization.

Reaching his full potential didn't require him to suddenly stop being goofy, or *ever* stop, for that matter. It only urged him to stop operating within his comfort zone, incessantly. It was Edward's playfulness and general ease with which he moved through life that made him experience joy. Joy was what everyone strives for and rarely attains. Not that Edward was blissfully ignorant; on the contrary. He had been simply uninvolved externally and relatively self-absorbed, in the most non-egocentric sense.

Skipping and hopping along the sidewalk, avoiding puddles and people, Edward occasionally let out an "ow" or an "ouch" under his breath as his ankle stung or rubbed against his boot just enough to remind him of his place in the world. It was wintry enough to see even the slightest exhalation as a large puff of steam against the black evening backdrop punctuated with glimmering lights of shops and cars.

As he approached the hospital, he spied Clotilde shivering with her hands thrust deep into her pockets and her shoulders raised to her ears, looking from side to side, waiting to see Edward. This somehow pleased him. He stood there for a few seconds just observing her; she looked slightly frustrated, impatient, frowning a little, and yet Edward was captivated by her pink nose and the steam she was puffing out of her mouth with each frigid exhalation.

He waited long enough and as he went to step off the sidewalk, he didn't look at the traffic. A car's horn startled him and he took a step back. It also alerted Clotilde, who instantly looked in his direction. Her curious, frozen expression suddenly turned compassionate yet sultry, the moment they locked eyes. Clotilde gave Edward a welcoming smile, and he looked both ways in an exaggerated manner before crossing the street, still skipping, which made him wince as he irritated that troublesome spot on his ankle.

"Hi!" said Clotilde with her eyes twinkling, "Is something wrong with your leg? You look like you're limping?" She leaned in and kissed Edward just to the right of his lips as she spoke. Edward kissed the air.

They immediately started walking towards the restaurant at Edward's regular pace, and although Clotilde was tall, she had to run a few steps every so often to keep up.

"Yeah, I banged my ankle on the coffee table doing karate," Edward admitted humbly.

"Oh! You know karate?"

"No."

There was a lengthy, serious pause. Then they both laughed, and laughed harder the more they thought about it.

"Edward, you're so funny!" Exclaimed Clotilde as she wiped a near-frozen tear from the outer corner of her eye.

"Oh sure, laugh at my inadequacies. I'll have you know, missy—" He jested, but Clotilde cut him off simply by looping her arm in his, hugging it and putting her ear to his shoulder all in one swift motion. She giggled. "You'll have me know what?"

Edward was so taken aback, and he didn't know how to finish his sentence. "I don't know. I really don't know what I was going to say. My ankle pain is clearly interfering with my brain function." Clotilde just giggled more. It wasn't a ditsy giggle; it was a very intelligent giggle filled with a sense of deep knowing.

The tantalizing fragrance of warm buttery herbs and garlic welcomed them as they arrived at the entrance to the restaurant when a thought suddenly struck Edward, and he stopped short of the door. He unhooked Clotilde's arm from his and moved her in front of him, holding her forearms.

"Is something wrong?" Clotilde looked very concerned as she tilted her face up to Edward's. He took a few moments to formulate his thoughts and maintained a stoic expression that flustered Clotilde, but Edward was too flustered himself, to notice.

"I just realized something." He took another long pause.

Clotilde was colder now that she wasn't moving and started to jitter. "Which is...?" She waited. "Maybe we could go inside?"

Edward held her in place, squarely in front of him. "No, no, wait." He thought some more. "If I weren't so clumsy or careless, we wouldn't have met."

"You don't know that." Clotilde wasn't sure where Edward was going with this. "We could have met numerous ways, considering I work with your best friend's sister."

"No, I don't mean to belittle the importance of our meeting." He let out a deep sigh because he realized he wasn't formulating his thoughts in the most straightforward way.

"What I mean," he continued, "is that I did something unusual, which for starters was me going out alone, and then I did something careless, not so unusual, which then got me beat up and landed me in the hospital where I not only met you, but I also managed to get this potential serial date-rapist arrested and out of our workplace and... you know what I mean?"

Clotilde understood what Edward was saying but not quite sure where he was going with it. "I think so. Do you think it was a fluke, or do you think it was something else?"

Edward paused again and looked down. Clotilde turned her hands to grab Edward's arms as he was still holding her. She shook him slightly to gently urge him to continue.

"Everyone wants to strive for these huge things, to have these big ideas and plans and stuff." Edward stared down into Clotilde's face as her eyes widened with anticipation.

"But it's the same stuff that makes us idiots, that also makes us— ok maybe not *idiots*, but the stuff we think is wrong with us, and stuff we wish wasn't part of us. With a dash of out-of-character shit thrown in occasionally or destiny or synchronicity, and other crap like that. It's like, here we are just going along in our strange little lives, billions of us, and we each have these things about us that we think prevent us from reaching our dreams or our aspirations, or we fail to even have any or feel like we're supposed to have a single epic life purpose.

"But it's all the stupid, regular, daily, almost-accidental shit that makes us—" Edward fumbled with a variety of consonants in search of the right word to describe what he was trying to convey, and his waving hands were no help in his attempt to pluck the word from the air.

Clotilde leaned in; she knew exactly what it was. She pressed her cool cheek to his and whispered, contentedly, in his ear.

"Magnificent?"

"Yes."